D0978852

GUYS✦READ

THE SPORTS PAGES

Also available in the Guys Read Library of Great Reading

VOLUME 1—GUYS READ: FUNNY BUSINESS
VOLUME 2—GUYS READ: THRILLER

GUYS READ

THE SPORTS PAGES

EDITED AND WITH AN INTRODUCTION BY
JON SCIESZKA

STORIES BY

**DUSTIN BROWN, JAMES BROWN,
JOSEPH BRUCHAC, CHRIS CRUTCHER,
TIM GREEN, DAN GUTMAN,
GORDON KORMAN, CHRIS RYLANDER,
ANNE URSU, AND JACQUELINE WOODSON**

WITH ILLUSTRATIONS BY
DAN SANTAT

 WALDEN POND PRESS
An Imprint of HarperCollinsPublishers

Walden Pond Press is an imprint of HarperCollins Publishers.
Walden Pond Press and the skipping stone logo are trademarks and registered
trademarks of Walden Media, LLC.

GUYS READ: THE SPORTS PAGES

Library of Congress Cataloging-in-Publication Data is available.
ISBN 978-0-06-196378-0 (trade bdg.) — ISBN 978-0-06-196377-3 (pbk.)

Typography by Joel Tippie
12 13 14 15 16 LP/RRDH 10 9 8 7 6 5 4 3 2

First Edition

CONTENTS

BEFORE WE BEGIN . . .

I grew up with five brothers, and we played a lot of sports.

We played the big ones like baseball, basketball, football, and hockey.

We also played golf, tennis, lacrosse, soccer, bowling, Ultimate Frisbee, guts Frisbee, skateboarding, whiffleball, waterskiing, snow skiing, swimming, water polo, wrestling, boxing, rugby, bicycle racing, canoe racing, sailing, kayaking, rafting, rowing, Ping-Pong, billiards, horseshoes, bocce ball, motorcycle racing, car racing, demolition derby, fencing, snowshoeing, bow hunting, fishing, shooting, knife throwing, rock climbing, ice-skating, racquetball, volleyball, badminton, handball, squash, weight lifting, running, long jumping, high jumping, shot putting, javelin tossing, darts, croquet, floor hockey, underwater hockey, kickball, surfing, snowboarding, curling, wood chopping, arm wrestling, leg wrestling, and thumb wrestling.

With our friends and little brothers we also played sports we invented: Frisbee butt waterskiing, 360 spring hoop power dunk basketball, apple war, full-contact volleyball, BB gun biathlon, running hatchet toss, demolition sledding, bicycle polo, midnight ice sailing, tree jumping, log tossing, daredevil stunt rope swinging, group brawling, tree chopping, tree burning, speed pizza eating. . . .

In fact, now that I think of it, most of the things we did we turned into a sport, a contest, a competition. Even if it was a race to get into the car to go to church, we competed to see who was fastest, strongest, best.

So in keeping with that spirit of competitive sports, here is a collection of the fastest, strongest, funniest, wildest, and best sports stories. All written exclusively for Guys Read.

My son, Jake, an amazing athlete and long-suffering receiver of lame sports books, once wisely explained to me that just because a guy likes to play sports doesn't mean he likes to read about them.

That is so true.

But there is something about a good sports story that

is exactly like a good game. The good game and the good story both reveal character and truths bigger than the game or the story.

And like any good sport, a good sports story depends on teamwork. It needs a writer willing to give his or her best, and a reader willing to do the same.

Take a look at any one of the stories in this collection. There is everything from football to friendship to baseball to fighting, and a lot more in between.

This bunch of writers brought their best.

Now show us what you've got.

Jon Scieszka

HOW I WON
THE WORLD SERIES
BY DAN GUTMAN

The story I'm about to tell you is so amazing, so improbable, and so preposterous, you're going to think I must have made it up. But I swear every word of it is true. This is not fiction.

You may have heard that the Boston Red Sox lost the 1986 World Series to the New York Mets because a guy named Bill Buckner let a ground ball go through his legs.

It's a lie!

The truth is that the Red Sox lost that game because of *me*. Dan Gutman. I won the World Series that year.

That's every kid's fantasy, isn't it? It sure was when I was a kid. You're standing there at home plate. The bases are loaded. Your team is three runs down in the bottom of the ninth. Seventh and deciding game of the World Series. There are two outs. Full count. It all comes down to one pitch. The crowd is going crazy. It's all up to you.

And you hit a walk-off grand salami that wins it all.

It didn't exactly happen that way, but I do feel that I was responsible for the outcome of the 1986 World Series.

Let me explain.

The story actually starts a bit earlier. Well, a *lot* earlier— back on January 5, 1920. That was the day the Red Sox sold a twenty-four-year-old kid named Babe Ruth to the New York Yankees. Up until that point, the Red Sox were the kings of baseball. They'd won five of the first fifteen World Series. Ruth led them to the championship in 1916 and 1918. But after they sold him to the Yankees, the Red Sox would not win another World Series for *the rest of the twentieth century*. And the Yankees, who had never won a World Series before Ruth arrived in New York, would go on to win twenty-seven of them and become the most dominating team in baseball.

The Red Sox were cursed, it was said, because they'd sold Babe Ruth to the Yankees. It was called the "Curse of the Bambino."

It's not that Boston had lousy teams all those years. The

Sox were usually close to first place, but they always seemed to choke at the end. Twice they lost one-game play-offs to decide the American League pennant (1948 and 1978). Every time they made it to the World Series (1946, 1967, and 1975), they lost Game 7. It's almost as if the ghost of Babe Ruth was watching over Boston all those years, making sure the Sox never won it all.

What does any of this have to do with me winning the World Series? I'm getting to that. Be patient, will you?

Okay, it was the night of Saturday, October 25, 1986. I was not in Shea Stadium in New York City, where the World Series was taking place. I was at my brother-in-law's apartment in Princeton, New Jersey. That's how good I am. I didn't even have to be *at* the World Series to influence the outcome!

It was Game 6. Boston won the first two games, and the New York Mets won the next two. Game 5 went to the Sox, putting Boston ahead three games to two. One more victory and the Red Sox would be World Champions for the first time since 1918. The curse would finally be over.

Sixty-eight years. That's a long time to wait. People had been born, lived their lives, and died of natural causes since the Red Sox had last won. The last time the Sox were World Champions, there was a world war going on. The *first* one.

Personally, I never cared if the Red Sox won or lost. What I cared about was the New York Mets. I grew up in northern New Jersey, and I had been a Mets fan since I was ten. That's 1965, when they were just a few years old and really awful. I'm talking about laughably bad. Most of my friends rooted for the Yankees, who won the pennant every year and had superstars like Mickey Mantle and Roger Maris. Me, I like to root for underdogs.

So let's get back to the 1986 World Series. As I said, one more win and the Red Sox would be champs. Roger Clemens (24–4) was the Boston starter; Bob Ojeda (18–5) for the Mets.

In the top of the first inning, one of those "only in New York" moments occurred. Ojeda was about to throw a pitch when everybody began pointing up in the air at something. A yellow parachute was floating down into the stadium! No kidding! It had a LET'S GO METS banner trailing behind it.

The parachutist, an actor named Michael Sergio, landed near the pitcher's mound. He jogged over to the Mets dugout, slapped hands with pitcher Ron Darling, and was led away by the police.

That should have been a tip-off that this was going to be one of those games you'd remember for a long time.

Anyway, Clemens had a no-hitter through four innings. His fastball was clocked at ninety-five miles per hour or *faster* on twenty-seven pitches. Ojeda, never a power pitcher, looked like he was chucking bowling balls in comparison.

The Red Sox scored a run in the first and another in the second. The Mets tied it in the fifth. The Sox scored *another* run in the seventh. The Mets got it back in the eighth. By that time, both of the starting pitchers were out of the game.

It was in the eighth inning that yours truly started to influence the course of the game. In Princeton, I was watching it on TV with my wife, Nina, her sister Erika, and Erika's husband, Alan. Nina and Erika were not big fans and didn't much care one way or another who won. They only watched the game with us to keep us company. Alan rooted for the Yankees, so by definition he hated the Red Sox. But I was the lone Mets fan.

At the same moment that Lee Mazzilli of the Mets lined a single to right in the eighth inning, my wife, Nina, absentmindedly picked a grapefruit out of a bowl that was sitting on the coffee table. Why there was a grapefruit in a bowl on the coffee table is anybody's guess. But when Mazzilli came around and scored the tying run, we naturally dubbed it "the lucky grapefruit." Furthermore, as a group, we determined that Nina should hold the grapefruit for the remainder of the game.

Not that any of us were superstitious, mind you. But it certainly couldn't *hurt* to hold a grapefruit while watching a ball game, right?

So Nina held on to the lucky grapefruit, and the score remained tied at 3–3 after nine innings. The Red Sox, you recall, were leading 3–2 in games, so one run in extra innings could win the World Series for them and end the Babe Ruth curse. With every pitch, you could almost feel the tension through the TV screen.

Leading off the top of the tenth for Boston was Dave Henderson. In the American League Championship Series, the Red Sox had been down to their last strike when Henderson slugged a home run. Well, guess what? Henderson did it again! He clubbed an 0–1 fastball from Rick Aguilera off the auxiliary scoreboard in left field, and suddenly it was Red Sox 4, Mets 3.

I was beginning to think the lucky grapefruit wasn't so lucky after all.

Aguilera struck out the next two Sox, but Wade Boggs doubled and Marty Barrett singled to add another run. Red Sox 5, Mets 3.

In Princeton, we sank back into the couch. In New York, some Mets fans headed for the exits to beat the traffic out of Shea Stadium. But in homes, restaurants, and bars all over Boston, it was jubilation. People were already dancing in the streets. The Red Sox were actually going to win the World Series! The Babe Ruth curse was finally over.

NBC began setting up TV cameras in the Red Sox clubhouse. Cases of champagne were wheeled in. The players' lockers were draped with plastic to protect them from the spraying champagne in the celebration that was about to take place. The World Series trophy was brought in.

Now I was *convinced* that the only luck in the grapefruit was bad. How does that song go? "If it weren't for bad luck, I'd have no luck at all."

It was the bottom of the tenth inning now, and the Mets came up for their last, desperate licks. Calvin Schiraldi was on the mound for Boston. The first batter, Wally Backman, flied to left. One out. Keith Hernandez flied to center. Two outs.

Stupid grapefruit!

You get a limited number of outs in a baseball game. The Mets had just one left, and they were two runs behind with nobody on base. It would take a miracle at this point. The Red Sox players were standing in the dugout, ready to run out on to the field to start the celebration.

"Give me that !@#$% grapefruit!" I yelled at my wife.

Actually, I didn't say "!@#$%," because it's not a word. But I did say a word that we can't print here and you should never say out loud. Unless, of course, you're in an extremely stressful situation. Like, if it's the bottom of the tenth and your team is down to its last out in the World Series, and it's all because your wife is holding a grapefruit.

Anyway, I ripped the grapefruit out of Nina's hands and sank into my gloom on the couch. It was all over. If Nina hadn't been holding the stupid grapefruit, I thought logically, the Mets would be winning.

Gary Carter, the Mets catcher, stepped up to the plate. With a 2–1 count, Carter dumped a dinky single into left field. The Mets were still alive, barely. Even if Carter, a slow runner, could score, the Mets would still be losing by one.

"Keep holding the grapefruit," said my brother-in-law Alan. "Maybe it's only lucky when *you* hold it."

It made sense. I was the only real Mets fan, after all.

Kevin Mitchell was called on to pinch hit. Just one problem: Mitchell was already in the clubhouse, naked, making plane reservations for his trip home after the game. He threw his uniform back on and hustled out to the batter's box. Three pitches later, he poked a single to left. Carter stopped at second.

I held the grapefruit tightly.

Schiraldi got two strikes on the next batter, third baseman Ray Knight. Now the Mets were down to their last *strike*. Their season could be over on the next pitch.

But it wasn't. Knight blooped a single to center! Gary Carter scored! Kevin Mitchell advanced to third. It was 5–4, the Mets one run away from tying the game again.

"Nobody touches the grapefruit except me," I announced.

Three little singles in a row. The tying run ninety feet away. One of my favorite players, Mookie Wilson, at the plate for the Mets.

At this point, the Red Sox changed pitchers. In came Bob Stanley, also known as "Steamer."

I've seen a lot of baseball games in my life. But what followed was the most exciting at bat I've ever seen and one of the most exciting in baseball history: ten pitches that would determine the season. The crowd at Shea Stadium was on its feet and screaming the whole time. In Princeton, we were all freaking out.

Here's how it went. . . .

Pitch 1: High and outside, but Mookie Wilson was aggressive, took a cut, and missed. Strike 1.

Pitch 2: Ball one. 1–1 count.

Pitch 3: Ball two. Outside. 2–1 count.

Pitch 4: Foul ball. Strike two. 2–2 count.

The Mets were down to their last strike *again*. A few of the Red Sox had one foot in the dugout and the other up on the field, ready to charge. The security police prepared to take control of the field to prevent a riot.

Pitch 5: Mookie just barely fouled off a breaking ball to stay alive. 2–2 count.

Pitch 6: Mookie fouled off *another* breaking ball. Still 2–2.

Pitch 7: Stanley tried to throw an inside fastball that would tail away from the batter, toward the plate. Just one problem—it didn't tail. The ball stayed inside, heading for Mookie's rib cage. He jackknifed to avoid getting hit—and the ball glanced off the catcher's mitt and bounced away!

"Go! Go! Go!" everyone was screaming. Kevin Mitchell scored from third standing up.

Incredibly, the Mets had tied the game. Ray Knight moved up to second on the wild pitch.

Nobody could believe what was happening. I gripped the lucky grapefruit as if it were a precious gemstone. Nobody was going to get it from me now. They would have to pry it out of my cold, dead hands.

The Red Sox sat back down in their dugout. The NBC crew grabbed their equipment and dragged it out of the Boston clubhouse like the place was burning down. The Red Sox could actually *lose* this game now. Somewhere, the ghost of Babe Ruth was chuckling. And Mookie Wilson was still at the plate.

Pitch 8: The count was full now. Mookie had gone to the dugout to get a new bat. He used it to foul off *another* pitch, back behind the plate. The count was still 3–2.

Pitch 9: Mookie fouled off yet *another* pitch, a bouncer down the third baseline. 3–2 count.

Pitch 10: The last pitch of the game, and one of the most famous in baseball history. Stanley delivered a fastball on the inside corner. Mookie swung and . . .

"Little roller up along first!" shouted Vin Scully on NBC TV.

"Ground ball to first!" shouted Jack Buck on CBS Radio.

". . . and a ground ball, trickling; it's a fair ball!" shouted Bob Murphy on WHN.

Hold everything for a second. You gotta see this for yourself. Go on YouTube and search for Bill Buckner.

The first baseman was a veteran ball player named Bill

Buckner. An excellent hitter, he had been in the big leagues for eighteen years. But he had bone spurs and damaged ligaments in both of his ankles. Earlier in the season, a holy woman had sent Buckner a magic elixir she claimed would heal his sore legs.

Usually, a defensive specialist was brought in to replace Buckner in late innings. But not this time.

He was guarding the first baseline and playing deep, behind the bag. The ball bounced crazily, with a lot of spin on it, just fair. Buckner only had to move a step or two to the left to get his body in front of it.

Mookie Wilson was a fast runner. It looked like it was going to be a close play at first. Buckner didn't have time to get down on his knees to block the ball, the way first basemen are taught, if he wanted to field it and beat Mookie to the bag. Instead, he stooped down for it, his legs apart.

No matter what sport you play, I'm sure you've heard your coach tell you to "keep your eye on the ball." Well, *do* it. The ball bounced three times and then slipped under Buckner's glove and between his legs! He never touched it!

"It gets through Buckner!" yelled Vin Scully.

"An error by Buckner! The winning run scores!" shouted Jack Buck.

"The Mets will win the ball game!" yelled Bob Murphy.

"The Mets win! They win! Unbelievable!"

"Ahhhhhhhhhhhhhhhhhh!" we all screamed in Princeton.

"It was the lucky grapefruit!" I shouted, holding the oblate spheroid aloft in jubilation. We all hugged one another as if we had won the game ourselves.

After all, in a way we had.

The Mets had evened the series at three games apiece. Two days later, they came from behind *again* to win Game 7, and the World Championship. The Curse of the Bambino lived on.

The Mets owed it all, of course, to the lucky grapefruit. Now, you can argue that me holding the grapefruit had absolutely nothing to do with Buckner missing that ball. You can argue that it was a total coincidence. But *you* don't know what would have happened if I hadn't grabbed the grapefruit, do you? We'll never know what would have happened.

Poor Bill Buckner got all the blame, of course. Jokes were on the street almost immediately, the best of which were . . .

Q. What do Bill Buckner and Michael Jackson have in common?

A. They both wear a glove on one hand for no apparent reason.

Q. Did you hear that Bill Buckner slipped and fell onto the Boston subway tracks?

A. Yeah, but he's okay—the train went between his legs.

More seriously, it got to the point where Buckner couldn't walk down the street in Massachusetts without people making fun of him. He actually received death threats from angry Red Sox fans. Buckner eventually moved about as far away as possible—to Idaho.

The year after his big error, the Red Sox released Bill Buckner. He went on to play for the California Angels, Kansas City Royals, and ended his career—amazingly enough—back with the Red Sox. He retired in 1990 with an excellent .289 lifetime batting average, 174 home runs, 2,715 hits, 1,208 RBIs, and 183 stolen bases. And he won the National League batting title in 1980. After his playing career, Buckner went on to become a hitting instructor and minor-league manager. But the only thing that most people remembered about him was that one ground ball.

And me? Well, after my brief career as a grapefruit holder, my wife and I got a cat. And you know what we named him?

No, it *wasn't* Buckner. Nice try, though.

We named the cat Mookie.

* * *

You're probably wondering what happened to the lucky grapefruit. Well, I thought about donating it to the Baseball Hall of Fame, but I've visited there many times and have never seen any citrus fruit on display. I thought about eating it, but I don't even *like* grapefruit.

After about a week, the grapefruit had become lopsided and rotten. So Nina and I held it solemnly and ceremoniously dumped it in a garbage can. It had served its purpose nobly.

This story has a happy ending, in a way. In 2004, the Red Sox were down three games to none in the American League Championship Series against the Yankees. They came back to win it, and then went on to win their first World Series in *eighty-six years.* People in Boston were so moved that parents picked up their sleeping babies and held them up in front of the TV screen so they could witness the once-in-a-lifetime event.

It got even better. Just to be sure the curse was dead, the Sox won the World Series again in 2007. And do you know who threw out the ceremonial first pitch at their home opener the next season?

Bill Buckner. The fans gave him a four-minute standing ovation.

(Then, of course, the Red Sox returned to form in 2011 when they blew a nine-game lead with twenty-four games to play.)

So what can we learn from all this?

Nothing! What, you thought there was going to be some kind of moral or lessons in this book? Forget about it. It's just sports. Sometimes you win, sometimes you lose. And sometimes you lose for eighty-six years in a row.

But even if curses and superstition have nothing to do with it, I still say I won the World Series. Nobody can tell me otherwise.

So if you find yourself holding a grapefruit and your losing team suddenly starts a rally, hold on to the !@#$% grapefruit!

FIND YOUR FIRE
BY TIM GREEN

The center snapped the ball, and Jake pivoted one foot, tearing up grass and pulling out of the line, accelerating toward the other side of the formation. His target flashed in front of him from nowhere. The target was Bobby Lemke, Jake's best friend and the team's star defensive end. Bobby wasn't looking. If Jake smacked him hard enough, he could knock him into next year. It could be a classic trap block, something to make an offensive lineman drool.

Instead of unloading with a monster hit, Jake put his hands out and turned his head, bumping Bobby away from the hole where the runner should be zipping by in the next instant. Bobby twisted like a snake and clubbed Jake's shoulder with the back side of his hand as he cleared Jake's body and threw himself into the hole. Before Jake could turn around, he heard the cry.

"Fumble!"

The ball squirted between Jake's legs. He dove on it and felt the pile of bodies build up on his back as the cry for the ball spread through the team like a grass fire. Jake clutched the ball tighter than a mother holds her baby. In the dark, cramped space, Jake felt someone's hands slither into his arms and grab at the ball. Jake tugged, but the wicked fingers clawed for the ball with an iron will, twisting it free and yanking it from Jake's grip.

As the players climbed off the pile, the light revealed Bobby Lemke holding the ball high for all to see. A cheer went up from the defense. The scrimmage was over. Ten extra sprints for the losers. That was Jake, the loser.

Coach Heath grabbed Jake's face mask and pulled Jake's head close enough that Jake could feel the heat of his coach's breath.

"You had a clean shot to annihilate Bobby. Why didn't you?"

Jake shrugged because he couldn't explain it.

"You think he's your *friend*? There are no friends on the football field. Get it? He's on the other side. You want to win, you beat him into the dirt. That's the game." Coach

Heath looked around at the rest of the team, challenging anyone to say otherwise.

He turned back to Jake, disgusted, and let go of his mask. "And then you let him steal the fumble? Look at you, Jake. You're big as a horse, and you can hit like one, too. You got to find your fire, son. Without that, you're just another big tub of lard out here flopping around."

Coach blew his whistle, signaling the team to line up for sprints, then he stomped away.

Jake adjusted his shoulder pads and jogged to the line. After sprints, the team knelt in a tight knot around their coach, huffing and sweating.

"Just so you all know. Coach Commisso, the head coach from Immaculate Heart, is going to be at our intrasquad scrimmage on Saturday." Coach Heath looked directly at Bobby Lemke. The rest of the team knew why. "He told me personally that they've got one full scholarship left. Dirk Forester got one last year. You guys remember how good he was. And the last player from Eastview to go to IH is playing for the Cowboys, so you all know what it means."

Jake knew the Cowboys lineman Coach Heath was talking about, as did any kid growing up in Eastview who cared one bit about football. He also knew that IH was a football factory, a perennial contender for the state high school championship. Most of the players at IH ended up playing in college, many of them Division I. Jake stretched his neck to peek at Bobby Lemke through the small army of pads. Sprigs of blond hair sprouted out from the back of Bobby's helmet. His big, sad eyes gave him the look of a hound, and his smile uncovered teeth as crooked as old fence posts.

Jake was the only one who could lay claim to being Bobby's best friend, but everyone liked him, and everyone was rooting for him to get that scholarship. Bobby's dad wasn't around anymore, and his mom was one of the thousands who'd lost her job when the GM plant shut down. He didn't have money for a hot lunch, let alone the hefty tuition it cost to attend Immaculate Heart.

Jake had a dad who owned an electronics distribution company. They lived in Crestline Hills, a gated community. His mom didn't work and never had to. Jake's two older sisters had gone to IH, and Jake would enroll next spring, paying the full freight like most of the wealthy students who went there. Jake and Bobby planned on being teammates for the next ten years, finishing up at Eastview Junior High, then four years at IH before spending their next four or five either at UT, Notre Dame, USC, or Alabama. They'd make that decision after they visited the campuses, which they also planned on doing together.

Their only problem was going to be the pros. They hadn't figured out how to rig that yet, although Bobby pointed out that if they weren't drafted by the same team, they'd both be free agents after their first four years in the league. With lofty goals like that, Coach Heath's comment about Jake being just another tub of lard made him scowl as he trudged toward the locker room.

As an offensive lineman, Jake didn't think he needed the maniacal intensity of a defensive player like Bobby. Jake was the biggest eighth grader he'd heard of—six feet one inch, 244 pounds—and the doctor said he wasn't finished growing. He figured that size, and some pretty nimble feet, should allow him to skate into the NFL, but Coach Heath's burning face suggested there was something else he might need.

"Sorry about the fumble." Bobby laughed and smacked him on the butt halfway across the parking lot.

"What's wrong with you?" Jake aimed a scowl at Bobby.

Bobby's face fell and he shrugged. "I don't know. It's football."

"Yeah, I guess." Jake knew Bobby had already found his fire, and that it burned out of control. "You want to come over and swim? My mom's grilling steaks."

Bobby scratched up under his shoulder pads. "I love a steak."

They changed out of the sweaty practice gear and biked over to Crestline Hills wearing shorts, T-shirts, and their purple-and-white Eastview Football caps backward to keep them from flying off. Jake waved, and they passed through the guard gates barely slowing down. Jake's family lived in a big brick house with towering white columns at the top of a tall hill. Jake and Bobby parked their bikes just inside the garage next to the Range Rover.

"Man, I can't wait to be rich." Bobby ran a finger along the Range Rover's sleek hood line. "I'm getting a black one of these when I get my first-round signing bonus."

"Money doesn't really matter." Jake looked around the garage at the gleaming cars and really believed it.

Instead of going through the house, they headed straight for the pool, where the smoke from grilling steaks floated up from the outdoor cook station, making their mouths water. They changed into bathing suits in the pool house—Bobby used an extra of Jake's—and dove in. They splashed over to the waterfall and let the water pound their heads, laughing as it sent them plummeting down.

At the basketball hoop near the shallow end, they began a game of one-on-one. Jake had an outside shot, but the rebounds and the inside game all belonged to Bobby. After a missed three-pointer, Jake and Bobby both dove for the ball. Jake got his hands on it first, but Bobby tore it loose like a pit bull on a bone, swinging elbows and hair until Jake felt a sharp pain in his nose and let go.

"Ha!" Bobby turned and dunked one home.

Jake stood holding his nose. He held up his hand for Bobby to see the wash of blood.

"Dude, I'm sorry. Wow. Man. Did I do that?"

"No, I threw my face into your elbow to teach you a lesson. Of course you did it!"

"Yeah. Man. Sorry."

Jake turned away, sulking. Bobby put a hand on his back.

"Come on, dude. You know I love you."

"That's weird."

"Don't go soft on me. You know what I mean."

They both laughed. Jake's nose shut down, and they didn't get out until Jake's mom called to them from the screened-in porch above. They dried off quickly and raced up the steps past Rosalita with the platter of steaks, nearly knocking her down. She scolded them in Spanish.

They sat at the table with eager looks. Jake's mom greeted them and sat sipping a glass of white wine and looking nervously into the kitchen until Jake's dad swept out onto the deck, loosened his tie, and tossed his suit coat over the back of his chair. Jake's father was a big man, but in the last year, he'd grown thin. His hair had gone gray, and the lines on his face had deepened. Things were always quieter when Jake's dad was around, but the tight skin around his jaw and the way he gnawed at his steak made everyone even more uncomfortable.

Even Bobby picked up on the dark mood, and he excused himself before Rosalita brought out the apple pie. Bobby never missed dessert. Jake's father followed Bobby with his eyes until Jake's friend disappeared around the corner of the house near the garage.

Jake's father cleared his throat. He took Jake's mother's hand in his own, but directed his eyes at Jake.

"I'm going to meet this head-on, Jake, and I want you to as well. We've got problems. Serious problems. With money."

Jake smiled and looked from one parent to the other for signs of a joke. His father never talked about money. Money was something they always had, and lots of it.

"My company is . . . the bank . . . we're closing up. We're going to have to move."

Jake nearly gagged. He shook his head. "Not now. Not this season."

His father took a deep breath. "We'll try to find a place in the district so you won't have to change schools this year, but after that, I can't make any promises. I'm going to have to start over, and I don't know if this is the right place to do it."

In his mind, Jake could see the wrought iron gates you had to drive through to enter Immaculate Heart, the winding road up through the trees, and the clock tower atop the main building. It was the next chapter in his life. They all knew that. It had to be. They were a state powerhouse, and Coach Commisso was known for grooming players into Division I–caliber stars.

"But wherever we live, next year I'll be going to IH anyway, right?" The words sounded dream-like and hollow to Jake, even though he was certain they'd come from his own mouth.

His parents looked at each other.

His father winced. "I don't want you to get your hopes up, Jake."

"But you can live anywhere. Remember Sue's friend? Her family was out in Huffton." Sue was Jake's sister, and her best friend traveled an hour each way just to attend IH.

"It's not getting there." Jake's mom spoke softly. "You're not listening. IH isn't something we're going to be able to *afford*, Jake. We're all going to have to make sacrifices. Eastview's public school is fine. And if we move out of town, we'll find another good place."

"But . . . football."

"Maybe next year we could find a place in Lawtonberg," his mother said. "They have some reasonable homes, and a good high school team, right?"

His dad's face crumpled. "Did you hear what I said? We're talking about the business I built up from nothing. You're worried about high school football?"

Jake stabbed at a chunk of apple and dug it free from his pie without eating it. "Sorry."

"We're all going to be fine." His mother flashed a smile across the table at them.

The sweetness and light in her voice filled Jake with dread. That's how it worked with her: the sweeter she sounded, the worse things really were. Jake excused himself.

"Where are you going, Jacob?" His dad growled like Jake was jumping ship or something.

"Let him, Frank. He loves that football."

Jake jogged upstairs and threw himself on his bed. If it even was his bed anymore. Did it belong to the bank now? He wove his fingers through his hair and pulled until it hurt. He remembered his words to Bobby about being rich not mattering, and he screamed into the pillow. When he said that to Bobby, he was talking about cars. The kind of car you drove didn't matter, but going to IH? That mattered. How could he *not* go to IH? They said you could make things happen by visualizing them. If that were true, he *had* to get into IH.

Jake didn't get online. He didn't play Xbox. He didn't text anyone. He sat staring at the wall before he got up and ran his fingers over the framed pictures of all the football teams he'd played on since he was six. That brought him to his trophies. He held the smooth, cool figures to his lips—not to kiss, but to truly feel them and remember the sweat and pain he'd suffered to help earn them.

The final and biggest trophy was from last year's Junior High District Championship. Jake turned it over in his hands, then took the picture off the wall behind it, remembering last year's eighth graders who'd gone on to high school. He smiled at the way he and his classmates had changed so much in just one year. Last year, Bobby's hair was gone with a buzz cut. Jake's had been longer, so that his straight brown hair hung down into his eyes like a shaggy dog's.

His gaze went back and forth between Bobby and Dirk

TIM GREEN

Forester. Dirk went to IH. Like Bobby, Dirk lived in the apartment complex next to the Wal-Mart. Like Bobby, Dirk had been a wild man on the field, but Dirk was not as nice off it. Dirk was at IH. Bobby would be at IH. Jake's stomach twisted as he wondered where he would be.

He studied Bobby's face. It didn't look so mean. Bobby was fun, and funny, almost laid-back—but on the field? Jake rolled his eyes and picked at the dried blood crusted at the edge of his left nostril. Something happened to Bobby on the football field, or even in a stupid game of pool basketball. He was a different person, a person with fire in his belly, in his brain.

Jake looked at his own face in the picture, framed by the long, dark hair. He didn't see any fire. He put the picture back on the wall and went into his bathroom—would he have to share a bathroom in their new home? He stared into the reflection and his blue eyes, deep into the dark pits at their centers. He thought about staying behind, being left at Eastview and its mediocre high school football team coached by a gym teacher whom no one liked but who kept the job because his father was president of the school board. If Eastview's varsity had a winning season, it was considered a huge success. If IH didn't *win the state title*, its players and coaches hung their heads in utter defeat.

The thought of staying behind, or even of moving to a decent school like Lawtonberg, made him sick. He stared harder into his own eyes and thought he saw something. A spark.

Jake grit his teeth. A low growl crept up out of his throat.

Why should he have to stay behind? It made him sick. It made him . . . mad.

The spark became a flame. He sneered at himself.

"What am I going to do?" His voice sounded to him like a crying girl's. Daddy can't pay for IH. Boo-hoo . . .

"You big baby!" Jake snarled at himself. "No one says that scholarship belongs to Bobby Lemke. You want it? Take it!"

Jake couldn't concentrate on any of his lessons, even English, his favorite subject. The words seemed to spill from his teachers' mouths like drool, meaningless and unpleasant.

Jake couldn't get stuck in Eastview, playing for a varsity coach everyone knew was a joke. If the coach was a joke, the team was a joke, and the players were treated like jokes. Even moderately talented players moved into districts like Lawtonberg's—a team that was no stranger to the state play-offs—if they could.

Still, nothing compared to IH.

When the final bell rang, Jake mustered up his courage and walked into Coach Heath's classroom. Coach taught science. Jake didn't have him for a teacher, but they were doing the same thing in Jake's class: dissecting frogs. Coach stood bent over a lab counter next to a thin kid with pale skin, messy black hair, and a red NASCAR T-shirt. The kid looked up and blinked through thick glasses.

"Jake," Coach asked, "what's up?"

Jake looked down at the frog, pinned to the tray on its back and sliced open down the middle of its belly. Jake swallowed.

"Can I talk to you, Coach?"

"I'm helping Gene with his lab, then I've got a minute before practice. Stick around. Did you do your frog yet?"

Jake shook his head, then nodded.

"Which is it?" Coach asked.

"We did it, but we worked in groups. I recorded the findings."

"Like the group secretary, huh?"

"I guess."

Coach nodded without trying to hide his disgust. "That's why I make everyone do their own."

"Here, look." Coach used his stubby fingers to peel back

the frog's belly, exposing a maze of guts.

Vomit bubbled up into the back of Jake's throat.

"Yeah, see? You don't like to look, but that's how you learn. Here. See this? That's the heart. The center of it all. How can you understand how it all works if you don't see it up close and personal?"

Coach seemed to be enjoying Jake's discomfort. Gene poked the rubbery lungs with his own bare finger, then used tweezers to scoop up a strand of intestines that looked like a waterlogged worm. Jake turned away.

Coach chuckled and wiped his hands. "All right, come over to my desk. Gene, take out the major organs we talked about in class and label them. I'll show you how I want them weighed when we're done."

Jake followed the coach to his desk and sat down in the chair off to the side. He clasped his left arm with his right hand and leaned forward so he could talk quietly.

"Coach, I want to move from guard to tackle."

Coach Heath's eyes widened. A smile crept onto his face. "You sniff a little too much formaldehyde?"

Jake furrowed his brow.

"That's the embalming fluid they pickle those frogs in." Coach nodded toward the lab counter. "Sometimes it makes people loopy."

"No, I want to play tackle."

"You mean the position I've been trying to get you to play for the past two years?"

Jake nodded. "Left tackle."

"Left tackle?" Coach bit his lower lip, then he sighed and his shoulders slumped. "Jake, I know you and Bobby are friends, but are you really going to embarrass yourself like this just to help him get a scholarship to IH? Don't you have *any* pride, son?"

Jake squinted. "What? What do you mean?"

Coach tilted his head. "You think I don't know? That you'll lie down for Bobby in the scrimmage with the IH coach so he can walk all over you. It's just not right, Jake, for you to make a fool out of yourself. I don't think Bobby needs the help. He does a pretty good number on Collin Mettler as it is."

Jake blinked. "I'm not doing it for Bobby, Coach. I want to do it for *me*. I want to go to IH, too. You said the head coach will be watching. I want to play there."

"But you don't need a *scholarship*, son."

Embarrassment burned Jake's face, but he shrugged it off. "You said I got to find my fire. Well . . ."

"So, you're gonna find your fire by having Bobby Lemke beat the tar out of you in front of the IH coach? You see what he does to Mettler every day."

"I just think . . ." Jake's voice faded off.

"Think what?" Coach Heath dipped his head so he met Jake's eyes.

Jake hesitated. He looked up and directly into Coach Heath's eyes. "I can take care of him."

"You can, huh? You feel confident about that? You'll be up against Bobby every day for the rest of the season."

"I know I can."

Coach chuckled again. "Well, I guess we'll see about that. Yeah, Jake, I'll move you to left tackle. That's where you belong anyway. But you're there for the scrimmage, too. If I make this move, I'm not going to change it. Mettler's not a great player, but no one deserves to be a yo-yo. Don't ask to switch back."

"I want to be there for the scrimmage."

Coach nodded. "Okay. Fine."

Jake didn't chatter with his teammates in the locker room, and when Bobby slapped him on the rump on their way to the field, Jake said nothing. When the time came for one-on-one drills with the offensive linemen battling the defensive linemen, Jake took his spot at left tackle.

Bobby snorted. "What are you doing?"

"I'm left tackle now."

Bobby gave him a confused look, then he shook his head and got down in his stance. "Okay, you asked for it."

Coach Heath moved the big tackling dummy into position about five yards behind the center, then he walked over to where Jake faced Bobby.

"You two set?" Coach clamped his whistle between coffee-stained teeth and narrowed his eyes with expectation. "On your movement, Jake."

As the offensive lineman, Jake got to make the first move. He swallowed back the flutter in his chest and took a smooth backward step, cutting off Bobby's outside angle to the quarterback. In the same instant, he coiled his arms for the two-handed punch he'd try to deliver to Bobby's chest.

Bobby barreled straight at him.

Jake saw stars at the collision. He stepped back again, and again, punching and keeping his hips low. Bobby's right hand found its way up and under Jake's face mask, clawing at the soft flesh of his mouth and nose. Instead of wincing and lilting, Jake punched hard and found a grip under the edge of Bobby's shoulder pad. He sensed the bag directly behind him. He'd given up as much ground as he could.

Jake roared, lifting and wrenching at the same time.

Bobby crossed his legs, and he went over sideways. Jake followed him to the ground, free-falling on top of him with every ounce of his 244 pounds. The air grunted from Bobby's lungs. He thrashed beneath Jake, trying to get up. Jake accidentally got poked in the eye and cried out. Yesterday Jake would have skittered away from the pain.

Today he ate it up, growled, and kept Bobby pinned down. Coach's whistle split Jake's ears. Hands from all quarters grabbed at him and pulled him free from Bobby, who sprang to his feet, snorting and flailing and spraying sweat across Jake's face. Coach hammered the whistle and stepped between them.

"Enough! Good, I like it. Good battle. That's how you fight!" Coach gave them both a final shove, separating them even farther. "Next up."

Bobby glared at Jake, growling while the rest of the linemen took their turns. When it was his and Jake's turn to go again, Bobby came at him like a maniac.

Jake won again. He lost the next round, though, when Bobby struck, then spun, disappearing like a genie and crashing into the bag. Jake struck his own helmet, and it was the last time that day Bobby beat him. During run drills, Jake got his pads lower than he'd ever done before. He fired out quicker, pumped his feet faster, and matched every bone-jarring hit with one of his own.

At the end of practice, Bobby waited until they were in the locker room, outside of Coach's hearing, before he grabbed Jake and slammed him up against a locker.

"What are you *doing*?" Bobby's breath was hot with tuna and onions.

Jake gripped Bobby's hands without tearing them free. He looked around at the rest of the team, who had stopped moving and were staring at them. "Playing football."

"That's not how *you* play."

"It is now."

"You do that tomorrow, and I will kill you, Jake. I will smash your face in."

Jake cast Bobby's hands aside and opened his locker. He ignored the stares and whispers and Bobby glowering at him from two lockers over. After he'd changed, Jake marched out of the locker room with his head high and biked back home.

He was in his room, just staring at the math problems in front of him, when his mom came in. "Bobby's here. He can stay for dinner if you like."

"Where is he?" Jake studied his mom with suspicion.

"Out back." His mom walked out as if nothing was wrong. To her, there obviously wasn't.

Bobby sat in a deck chair beside the pool with his arms folded tightly across his chest.

"What?" Jake didn't sit down.

"Seriously, what are you doing?" The edge and anger were gone from Bobby's voice.

"You make me look bad, and it's football." Jake clenched his hands. "I make you look bad, and something's wrong?"

"I can't be messing around like this tomorrow." Bobby's eyes flashed. "That IH coach will be here, and I need to look good. I can't have my best friend going all superhero on me."

"So, stop me." Jake folded his arms across his own chest.

"I thought we were going to IH together." Bobby's voice softened. "Are you kidding? What's wrong with you? You've got everything." Bobby nodded toward the pool, then the big house. "This IH scholarship is my ticket. You want to battle it out every day, compete with me to get better, fine. Do that *after* tomorrow."

Jake looked out over the rippling water and blinked at the sparkles. He wanted to explain, to tell Bobby what his father had told him the night before, but the shame of it all tackled the words in his throat. "Just play, Bobby. No one said this scholarship was going to come easy."

Bobby hung his head so that a curtain of blond hair

fell around his eyes. "Remember Fritzgelden and Stinson? What they did to you, or tried to do?"

Jake felt his cheeks burn, and it wasn't from the last rays of sunlight. "So?"

"You were going to quit football. Remember? They had you so scared . . ."

"So, you helped me and we're friends."

"I *saved* you. No one else would. They were going to tape you up and make you eat dirt."

Jake tried to see through the curtain of hair. Bobby didn't have to say that Jake had cried. They both knew he had, and it made Jake sick to even think of the two eighth-grade bullies from last year.

"So, now you own me? I'm your puppet or something?"

Bobby looked up, and the sun's rays electrified his blue eyes. He stood. "No, just my friend. That's what I thought, anyway."

Jake watched him go, slack shouldered and weighted down by disappointment and misunderstanding. At dinner, it was just he and his mom. His dad had to fly to Chicago. His mom asked him what was wrong.

"Everything." He kept his voice down to avoid an alarm. He didn't need any drama. He needed to get to sleep. The scrimmage started at ten. He said good night and kissed

40

her cheek. She squeezed his hand as he walked out of the room.

Jake tossed in a sweaty tangle of sheets most of the night. He woke up with the bright sun casting thick beams onto his bed, and he woke up tired. His mom made him breakfast and said, "Good luck."

She had no idea.

Jake pedaled to the school—empty on a Saturday morning—and locked his bike. He kept his eyes on the ground and built a small fire in his gut, fueling it with anger and desire. Bobby walked into the locker room, and Jake sensed his presence like a dark and silent thundercloud creeping up over a hilltop. He taped his wrists, then wiggled his fingers into padded lineman gloves. His shoulder pads smelled of dried sweat and dirt. The snaps on his helmet sounded like the distant gunfire of a battlefield.

Jake pushed through the locker room without a sideways glance. He didn't even see his teammates. His vision went inward, and his eyes glittered in the blaze. When he saw the IH coach in the stands with a foam cup of coffee and a clipboard, Jake's breakfast tried for a speedy retreat. A bit of vomit burned his mouth before he could swallow it down. He turned away and got his muscles loose.

Whistles blew. They ran. They stretched. They went through the banging and popping of pregame ritual, then the offense and the defense jogged to opposite sides of the field. The scoring system didn't matter to Jake. It wasn't about the offense winning the scrimmage. It was about him manhandling Bobby Lemke, pounding him into submission in front of the IH coach.

When he lined up across from his best friend on the first play, Bobby muttered, "Don't do this, man."

Jake answered by firing out with all the force he could muster, smashing heads with Bobby, driving his paws up under Bobby's pads, and driving his feet like a paint-can shaker. Jake wheeled his butt at the last instant, and the runner slipped through the open space. Someone hit Jake from behind, cutting his knees and sending him to the bottom of a big pile of bodies. He took Bobby down with him.

Bobby got up and glared at Jake. "Bring it."

The next play was a pass. Bobby raced around the outside, slapping Jake's hand, darting past him, and crashing into the quarterback. Bobby howled at the sun, and his defensive teammates swarmed him like a liberating hero.

Jake clenched his teeth and hands. He got back into the huddle, the flames now burning out of control.

The battle went on. Blood spilled. Sweat flew. Flesh got

clawed up like hunks of sod, leaving bloody divots on both their arms and lower legs. When it was done, Jake's head spun, and he staggered to the cluster of players surrounding their coach, vaguely aware that the offense beat the defense by a narrow point margin. He removed his helmet and knelt down. He had no idea if he'd beaten Bobby or if Bobby had beaten him.

Coach Heath introduced Coach Commisso from Immaculate Heart. Coach Commisso had a thick black crew cut and eyebrows. A shadow of stubble shaded his face. He cast an iron gaze out over the team. Jake pulled up a handful of grass and stared at the back of Bobby's sweaty head and the dark crescents of matted blond hair.

Coach Commisso said, "I like what I saw just now, and I know why you guys usually win your district. Good work, boys. As you know, we like to offer scholarships to IH to four young players every year. It's a full ride to a very prestigious academic institution."

Coach Commisso shared a secret smile. "And we've got a pretty good football team, too."

Everyone laughed politely.

"There's a lot of talent out here, I'll say that. You." Coach Commisso's eyes locked onto Jake. Everyone turned to look at him, and Jake's stomach knotted up tight.

"Jake," Jake said. "Jake Simpson."

"Jake. You've got a lot of promise. Great feet for a big man . . . and I like . . . I like your fire."

Jake couldn't tear his eyes away, but he sensed Coach Heath nodding his head.

"I could see you at IH one day."

Jake's chest tightened. He realized he'd forgotten to breathe. He forced himself to inhale and gasped.

"I'm gonna keep an eye on you. Sometimes we'll have a kid that doesn't work out, and then you could join your teammate here." Coach Commisso angled his head toward Bobby.

The team cheered. Bobby just stared at the coach. His chest heaved. He gulped the air, still trying to catch his breath from the scrimmage.

Tears blurred Jake's vision. He looked away and sniffed them back. The fire sputtered. Coach Commisso was talking about Bobby, but Jake wasn't hearing him. The flame distracted him, steady now, hypnotic. In a daze, he held up his helmet and chanted with his team, changed in the locker room, and left the school without a word.

He rode for half an hour without knowing where he even was. When he looked up, he saw a sign: LAWTONBERG 5 MI. Jake kept going. The next sign said 2 MI., and the flame

44

inside him crackled and grew. Jake soaked in the saltbox houses crammed together along old, tree-lined streets. A yard sign read: GO HUSKIES.

He saw the speed zone for a school and pedaled faster. The school's dusty brick walls baked in the Saturday morning sun. The soft tweet of whistles reached over the building from the football field beyond. Jake circled the school, dodging broken glass and a rusted muffler that lay dead by the curb. The bark of coaching mixed in with the whistles.

Jake parked his bike and studied the playing field as he passed through the fence. The head coach had on a floppy hat worn by soldiers in the desert. He was a big man, a former lineman. Jake waited for a water break and walked out onto the field, extending a hand.

"Coach, I'm Jake Simpson. My family might be moving into the district next year. I'm a football player. Offensive line."

The coach went up and down his frame with a practiced eye, and a smile spread across his face. He shook Jake's hand and shouted to one of his players.

"Givens, come here."

The quarterback jogged over with the ball still in his hands.

"This is Jake Simpson." The coach directed the quarterback to shake Jake's hand. "Boy this big might be just what we need next season to shore up our line and get us that championship, don't you think?"

The quarterback named Givens grinned and nodded.

Jake looked past them both at the huge banner above the stadium.

HUSKIE PRIDE

In his mind, he could see it happening, all of it, and it was like gasoline on the fire.

MAX SWINGS
FOR THE FENCES

BY ANNE URSU

It wasn't as if Maximilian Funk didn't know that things were going to go badly. After all, there's no good that can come out of being a new kid in school, especially when you've just moved halfway across the country, especially *especially* in the middle of the year. Nothing says *Give me a wedgie and hang me from the flagpole* like waltzing into a new middle school in February at a time when there are no other new kids to hide behind.

He knew things were going to go badly. If he knew just how badly they were actually going to go, though, he would have faked some illness that would keep him out of school for the rest of the year. Like Ebola.

So Max slowly got ready for his first day at Willard Middle School, spending more time than anybody ever had trying to decide whether it would be better to wear a sweater and T-shirt or a sweater and button-down shirt. He just wanted to get it right. Max had spent his middle school life thus far working hard to be the sort of kid no one ever noticed, except perhaps to say "Oh, I didn't see you there." Because there were only two ways to get noticed in middle school, and Max was never going to be the kid who got noticed in a Good Way, like if he were a basketball stud or did something amazing like winning an ice cream–eating contest or solving one of Mrs. Bjork's extra credit word problems. So that left the Bad Way. Better not to be noticed at all.

When he got downstairs, his mom presented him with a Minnesota Twins cap, flashing him a huge I-know-I-ruined-your-life-but-I-bought-you-this-fabulous-hat-so-it's-all-better-now smile. "Now you'll look like a native," she proclaimed.

Max frowned. He did not wear baseball caps. Baseball caps only served to emphasize his ears. Which were already doing a fine job of emphasizing themselves.

"Mom," he said, not trying to keep the exasperation from his voice, "baseball hats are for jocks. I can't stride in there pretending I'm a jock." Middle school kids could smell posers like a T. rex could smell a lame triceratops. It was a biological fact.

"You *are* a jock!"

"I play *tennis*, Mom."

"That's a sport!"

"Trust me. It's not the same thing."

"Come on, honey. Don't be nervous. Everyone's going to love you."

"It's February, Mom. Nobody cares."

"Of course they care!" she said. "You have so much to offer them!"

Max tried to keep from rolling his eyes. Every mother thought her kid was extraordinary. By definition, at least 75 percent of them had to be kidding themselves.

"Anyway," she added, putting the cap on his head, "this town's nuts about baseball. Just tell everyone at school you're from Beau Fletcher's hometown. They'll think you're a celebrity!"

Max sighed. Beau Fletcher was the veteran All-Star third baseman for the Minnesota Twins, a two-time MVP, future Hall of Famer, and the greatest thing to come out of New Hartford, NY, ever. People in New Hartford said Beau Fletcher's name with this dazed reverence, like he'd invented soup or something. It didn't matter whether he was a nice guy or anything. All that mattered was that he hit a jillion home runs. After Beau donated some money to help rebuild Roosevelt High's athletic fields, there was a movement to rename the school after him. After all, what had Franklin Delano Roosevelt done for them lately? In New Hartford, Beau Fletcher mattered so much that the universe needed to make people who didn't matter at all just to keep everything in balance.

People like Max.

And then it was time to go. Max's dread followed him to the car. It huddled its overgrown body into the backseat and kicked Max's seat the whole way to school. It lurked behind him as he went up the steps to the school and through the doors and down the hallway following the signs to the main office. And then, right before Max went in, it wrapped him up in an icy, immobilizing embrace—and then disappeared suddenly, leaving him all alone.

And that's when everything changed.

Because in the main office stood a woman, and next to her was a girl. And she was the most beautiful girl Max had ever seen. The girl had long, thick, wavy hair like a mermaid might have. And it was a rich, dark red, the kind of color that should only exist in a Crayola box or maybe a very special kind of slushie. And her eyes, her eyes were green like emeralds. Or Kryptonite.

Max's ears flushed.

"This is your official new student buddy," the woman, who had apparently been talking for some time, said. "Molly Kinsman. She's in sixth grade too."

"Hi, Max," Molly said, smiling a smile that would need no orthodontia. "I'm going to show you your classes and stuff, okay?"

Max opened his mouth but couldn't come up with a response. This was the sort of girl who would never pay attention to him unless she was assigned to. Her eyes were so green. Who did they remind him of?

"Ready?"

"Catwoman!" he thought. Except he said it out loud. His mouth hung open.

The girl blinked. "What?"

"I mean, yes," Max said. "I'm ready. Thanks. Thank you. Ready, Freddie!"

He closed his mouth. Molly gave him a curious look, then led him around the school. She chatted as she showed him his locker, the gym, the library, the cafeteria. And Max just followed, nodding and grunting like an ape desperately trying to hide the fact that it'd just been body-switched with a sixth-grade boy. But, he reflected, at least nodding and grunting was better than babbling. If he started talking, who knows what ridiculous thing would come out of his mouth next?

Molly dropped him off at his homeroom. "So, come find me in the cafeteria at lunch, okay?" she said brightly. "You can sit with us."

And then she turned and left, her invitation hanging in the air.

Max stared. Did she really want to hang out with him? Or was this just part of her job description?

Max sat through his first three periods wishing he were a different sort of person, the kind who might impress a girl like Molly, the kind who had anything interesting about him at all. If Molly thought he was cool, then surely the other kids would too. And then they wouldn't string him up on the flagpole by his underwear. There was a lot at stake.

Plus, then he'd get to hang out with her.

At lunchtime, he surveyed the cafeteria, and his eyes instantly found Molly's red head as if drawn there. His stomach flipped. *Don't blow it,* he told himself as he walked over. *This is your chance. Ready, Freddie.*

Molly was sitting at a table with a blond girl and a tall,

dark-haired boy. Max gulped. The boy looked like the wedgie-giving sort.

"Hi!" Molly said, smiling up at him. "Max, this is Jenny, and this is Logan. Guys, this is Max. He just moved here."

Max sat down and attempted to look interesting.

"Oh, do you like the Twins?" Jenny asked, nodding to his hat.

"Oh, well, you know," Max said, "my mom gave this to me. . . ." He cast a look at Molly. Should he play it like someone who loved baseball or someone who didn't really care that much? Was Jenny looking at his ears?

"Dude," said Logan, leaning in suddenly. "What position do you play?"

"Uh," Max looked around. Molly and Jenny were staring at him expectantly. "What do you mean?"

"What do I mean?" He nodded to Max's hat. "Baseball. Practice starts today!"

Of course. Logan was clearly a crazed jock who naturally assumed everyone around him was always thinking about baseball just because he was. Max looked at the girls but couldn't read them.

"Baseball?" he said. "It's February! There's snow on the ground!" There. That was a good, noncommittal answer.

"So?" Logan asked, looking at him as if he'd said fish

sticks were best when made out of people.

"The all-city sixth-grade tournament is coming up," explained Jenny. "We lost it last year. We're starting early."

Logan straightened. "*We* didn't lose anything. Last year's sixth graders did. But we're going to get it back this year. We have the best pitcher in the city."

"That's you, I assume?" Max said, half to himself. He knew this boy's type.

There was that look again. "Naw, dude. I'm shortstop. What about you?" He looked Max up and down in a way that reminded him of the way his mom picked out tomatoes in the grocery store. "We really could use a left fielder."

"Well, um, I don't really play baseball."

No one seemed to know what to say to that. Everyone suddenly looked down at their trays.

"I mean, I like baseball and everything," Max said quickly. "But I'm not very good at it. You know." He looked at Molly and laughed in what he hoped was a charmingly self-deprecating manner. "Everyone says I throw like a girl!"

The two girls turned their heads toward him slowly. Logan let out a long whistle.

Max grimaced. He'd just made himself sound like a total loser. "I mean," he said quickly, "I play tennis."

Logan blinked. "What?"

"Tennis. You know." He mimed a forehand for their benefit. Max actually had a very good forehand. But this is the sort of thing that's hard to show in mime.

Logan scrunched up his face. "My *mom* plays tennis."

Max did not know what to say. Many people's mothers played tennis. It did not mean there was something fundamentally wrong with the sport itself.

"Anyway," Logan said, "I gotta run to the library. See you later, Molly, Jenny. And"—he turned to Max—"you too, Venus!"

Max blinked. Oh. "More like Serena," he muttered defiantly.

Logan looked at him, and then a smile spread across his face, and it was the most delighted evil smile Max had ever seen—sort of like how Lex Luthor might look if he unwrapped a present Christmas morning and found the keys to global thermonuclear destruction.

"Right!" Logan said, laughing. "See you, Serena."

He left. Max looked at the two girls, who were distinctly not looking at him.

"Serena's better," Max explained.

And then silence, great and terrible, and Max felt himself fading into the wall, and along with it, all his prospects for a happy middle school life. Jenny shifted, then said she better go to the library too and got up and left, giving her friend a look that told Max that Molly was definitely hanging out with him because she was assigned to. He stuck his fork in his mac and cheese and attempted to jiggle it.

"So," Molly said after a pause, "where'd you move here from?" Her voice sounded flat. Max didn't understand. Was the tennis thing that dumb?

"Um, upstate New York. A little town called New Hartford. You've probably—"

Molly's eyes grew large. "That's where Beau Fletcher's from!"

Oh. Right. "Yeah, I know."

And then Molly looked up at him again. "Did you . . . know him?"

And there was that spark in her eyes again—Max might even go so far as to call it a glow. And it would be a terrible terrible thing to extinguish that glow again; why, Max didn't think he could live with himself.

"Know him? I mean." Max shifted. "Oh, well, I don't like to—"

As he talked, he was aware that his sentence was a runaway train picking up speed—but it didn't matter, for Jenny appeared again behind them just then to derail it.

"Hey, Molly," she said, "do you want a ride to practice after school?"

"Practice?" Max said, still choo-chooing on. "For what?"

Molly's eyes narrowed. "Um, baseball."

There are times in a boy's life when it is wise not to speak the words in his mind. But Molly's hair was the color of a cherry slushie, and Max was not wise.

"You go to watch baseball practice?"

Jenny exhaled. And the glow in Molly's eyes turned into something else entirely.

"I'm the pitcher," Molly said, each word an ice cube slipped down the back of Max's pants.

Jenny rolled her eyes. "The best one in the city," she added, and then sighed epically and stalked away. Molly glared at Max for another two beats, and then tossed her hair and got up and turned to go. Max's heart leaped out of his throat, followed by some words he didn't even know were there.

"He's my dad!" Max said.

Max froze. The words floated in the air. He blinked at Molly. Maybe she hadn't heard.

"Who's your dad?" she said, taking a step closer.

She'd heard.

Now, if you were sitting on the outside of this situation,

you would recognize this as the point where things could have been saved. But if you were inside it, you would see nothing at all to do but open your mouth and say:

"Beau Fletcher. Beau Fletcher's my dad."

Molly stared. And Max, Max stared too. Max's dad was not in any way, shape, or form Beau Fletcher. Max's dad lived in Poughkeepsie and franchised tanning salons.

Molly tilted her head and considered Max for one moment. Two. Max did not move. Inside, he could feel his intestines begin to unravel.

"You expect me to believe that?" she asked. But her voice didn't sound hostile. Just curious.

"I know," said Max. "It's really weird."

"But"—Molly's brow contorted—"Beau Fletcher's not married. He never has been. He's married to the game!"

Max nodded solemnly. "I know."

Molly's eyes widened, and then she too nodded, because she was a girl of the world. She sat down next to him. Max exhaled.

"So, why don't you have the same last name?" she whispered, leaning in to him so close Max could touch her hair. She smelled like cupcakes.

"Oh," said Max. "Well, you know, my mom raised me. He wasn't really around till I was a little older."

She gasped. "Does the school know?"

"Oh, you know." Max could not decide whether to nod or shake his head, so he jerked his head in a direction that could best be called diagonal.

"Wow," breathed Molly.

"So," Max said, blinking spasmodically. "Don't tell anyone, okay? It's really important." He cleared his throat. "It would be weird, you know?"

"Right," said Molly. "You don't want people to like you just because you're Beau Fletcher's son!"

"Right," said Max. *Just you,* he thought.

Molly stared at him as if expecting him to say more, and when he didn't, she just nodded as if she understood. His intestines curled back in place. Molly would never betray him. And her Catwoman eyes were fixed on him as if he himself had invented soup. Maybe the gods of middle school were finally smiling at him.

It was a little lie, that's all.

That night, Max went straight up to his room. He had work to do. He was no longer a boy-ape body-switch victim. He was a liar now, and that changed everything. Liars had information. They stuck as closely to the facts as possible. Liars kept in control of their words. And they did not ever ever ever babble.

This was going to be a challenge.

So he spent the evening reading up on Beau Fletcher. Nobody could talk about him without gushing over his stats: one jillion home runs, and a bazillion hits, and some crazy-high OPS, whatever the heck that was. It was like Beau was so amazing they had to make up a statistic for it. Most of the biographical stuff Max knew, of course—in New Hartford they taught Beau Fletcher history sometime between the alphabet and scissors. But buried in interviews were some interesting bits of information, things that brought out the picture of Beau Fletcher the man, the sort of thing you might know if he were your dad. Like he was scared of spiders. And he ate a pastrami sandwich before every game. And he was allergic to strawberries. And his favorite movie was *Wall-E*. In Minnesota, he was a spokesperson for milk, and even had his own ice cream flavor, which might be the coolest thing that could happen to a person ever. He could probably get it for free whenever he wanted, too, because they can't possibly charge you for your own ice cream flavor.

In short, Beau Fletcher was the sort of guy who, if you were going to have a famous guy for a dad, would be a great dad to have. Max was pleased.

*   *   *

He strode into school the next morning armed with everything there was to know about the life and times of Beau
Fletcher, in case Molly decided to quiz him on the finer
points of his dad's food allergies. But it wasn't Molly who
accosted him as he walked to first period. The hand that
grabbed his arm was Jenny's, her blond ponytail bobbing
determinedly behind her.

"Molly told me," she whispered, voice electric.

Max froze. "She did?" He turned slowly to look at her.

"I can't *believe* it!" Jenny said.

"You can't?"

Her blue eyes were sparkling. "No, I mean. It's *amazing*!
But you know"—she tilted her head—"you look like him a
little. Especially in the ears."

"Oh," said Max. "Look, Jenny . . ."

"I know, I know. I can't tell anyone. You don't want kids
to like you just because you're Beau Fletcher's son, right?"

"You promise?"

"Swear!" Jenny said, holding her hands up.

She disappeared into the stream of students then, and
Max tried to slow down his heart. Jenny believed him.
And, more importantly, Molly believed him. That's what
mattered.

He finally saw Molly at third-period English. She was waiting outside the classroom. For him.

"Hey," he said, because that is the sort of thing sons of baseball players say.

"Hi," Molly said. She looked around and then whispered, "I got a present for your dad."

"What?" His ribs abruptly cinched together.

"Yeah!" She reached into her bag and pulled out a little Wall-E pin. "I thought it could be, like, a good-luck charm, you know?"

"His favorite movie! How did you know?"

"I know everything about him! He's my favorite player of all time. Maybe he could wear it in the dugout someday so I could see? You could ask him that, right?"

"Right," Max said. "Sure!"

"Amazing," Molly said. "Oh, hey"—a look of regret crossed her face—"did Jenny talk to you?"

"Um." Max shifted. "Yes."

She tilted her head. "I'm sorry I told her. It just came up, you know? She's my best friend. I don't want to *lie* to her!" Her nose wrinkled up at the very thought.

"No, of course not!" Max said, wrinkling up his nose even more. "Just, um, don't tell anyone else, okay?"

"Oh, you don't have to worry about me," she said.

Max smiled. Of course she wouldn't tell. And if Molly told Jenny, Jenny was trustworthy too. And anyway, Molly wanted to hang out with him now. And that was worth anything.

Something changed in Max that day. For the first time in his life he was someone who was Someone, the sort of kid people noticed. In a Good Way. After all, if a girl like Molly believed he was the sort of kid who might have a baseball player for a dad, well, maybe that's who he was.

It would be something to have a major-league baseball player for a dad. And not just any major-league baseball player. Beau Fletcher, one of the best alive. It would have been the best thing ever. When Max was little, TC Bear would've come to all his birthday parties, and all the kids would think the Twins' mascot was his best friend. Beau would have taken Max to the ballpark all the time. Max would run around on the field, take grounders from the other players, drink Gatorade in the clubhouse, and tell all the kids in school about it the next day. Sometimes Max would bring his friends, too—but only sometimes. And his dad would go to his tennis matches whenever he could and cheer louder than all the other dads combined. And everyone would point and say, "That's Beau Fletcher! Cheering for his son! Tennis *is* a real sport!" But they'd still play baseball sometimes. Beau would pick Max up from school sometimes, and they'd stay afterward on the fields in the back of the school and have a catch as dusk slowly fell—father and son, night after night, just like it was supposed to be.

As Max walked through the hallways that day, he could feel himself standing taller, walking assuredly like Logan and all the other kids who mattered. And the funny thing was, it worked. By the end of the day he could feel the crackle in the air as the kids around him noticed him, sense them make way as he walked past, hear the staccato whispers and see the fingers pointing—

Uh-oh.

"Hey!" A boy from his English class grabbed him on the shoulder. "Do you think your dad could come to school sometime to autograph? I have baseballs like you wouldn't believe!"

"Um—" said Max.

"Man!" A girl with a unicorn on her shirt sidled alongside Max. "Your dad is, like, my favorite player of all time. I named all my gerbils after him. Do you think I could meet him sometime? I won't be weird!"

"Uh—" said Max.

"Serena!" Logan was standing in front of him, grinning.

"You were kidding when you said you couldn't play, right? You gotta come to practice. Hey, think your dad might come? Give us some tips?"

And that's what it was like as Max made his way through the throngs of adoring Beau Fletcher fans to his locker. He grabbed his jacket, then looked inside his locker as if it might be a very nice place to stay for a while.

"Hey!" Molly appeared behind him, looking very happy.

He stared at her, pale and shaking. "Everybody *knows*!" he whispered.

Molly let out an exasperated sigh. "Oh, Jenny! Gosh, she always does this! You can't tell that girl anything!"

Max blinked at Molly. Everything inside him was blank, a pocket of nothingness floating in endless space.

"Don't worry about it. Listen." She leaned her head toward him, voice thick with excitement. "I want to meet him."

"You do?"

"Please?" She put her small, pale hand on his arm. Max almost gasped. "He could help me with my changeup! We could just meet. You can do that, right?"

Max's stomach was a pit of boiling tar, and all his innards were slowly descending into it. "Molly, he wants it to be a secret—"

"I know, but it's just me. Tell him I'm the only female baseball pitcher in the sixth-grade tournament. Won't he think that's cool? Anyway, he must want to meet your friends. Doesn't he?"

"Molly, um, he's so busy, and—"

She looked at him, her eyes not exactly losing their glow but shifting a bit. "You mean you can't set up a dinner with your own dad?" She blinked. "Why not?"

Max froze.

"Molly!" The word exploded out of his mouth. One breath. Two. Oh, god. "I lied," he said finally.

She drew up. "What? What do you mean?"

This was it. This was his chance to come clean, to end this. And then he'd just be normal Max again, the kind of kid guys like Logan step on in the cafeteria, that girls like Molly never even think twice about. And this look she was giving him now—a little confused, a little hesitant, a little hurt, all because of something he'd done—no one would ever look at him this way again. He could write a poem about this look, if only he knew how to write a poem.

"I mean," he said, "I let you think something that wasn't true. Beau . . . my dad . . . he doesn't know about me. That's why we don't have the same last name."

Molly gaped. "Wow," she finally breathed.

"I know," he said, shaking his head with as much sincerity as he could muster. His lungs felt like they were about to crack into bits and puncture various vital organs. "They dated one summer. My mom was a lifeguard at the pool in college, you see. I guess they'd broken up by the time she found out she was pregnant. And by then he'd been drafted into the minors, and . . . my mom never told him. She raised me on her own." His breath slowed a little. This was good. This sounded plausible. Max was pretty sure he'd seen something like it on CBS once.

"I'm sorry I lied to you," he said, making his face as sincere as possible.

"It's okay," she said. "What matters is that you're telling the truth now."

Max could do nothing but nod.

"Does *anyone* know?" she whispered.

"No," he said. "Mom told everyone my dad was some guy in Poughkeepsie. I believed it most of my life."

"I can't believe it!" Molly bit her lip. "Don't you think he'd want . . . to know? I mean, if I had a son—"

Max just shrugged, as if this was the stuff of grown-ups and he could only wonder at it.

"I bet," Molly said, her face so close her hair brushed against his arm, "if Beau Fletcher met you, he'd just know.

He'd look in your eyes and see something. He'd *know*."

There was something buzzing in Max's ears now, and Molly sounded very faint. "Yeah. Maybe," he said. That would be something, wouldn't it? To look into your long-lost dad's eyes and see recognition there.

"Oh, Max," Molly said. She stared up at him. "Your story is incredible." And with that, she slipped into his arms and gave him a squeeze, as quick and magical as a fairy blink. And then she was gone. But Max, he did not move, not for a long time.

Max went home and planned on spending the weekend in quiet contemplation. There was a chance that it was over—that Molly, out of the goodness of her heart, would tell everyone to stop talking about it so Max would not have to feel bad about the dad he never knew. It was the sort of thing she would do. Eventually, it would all die down—and if not, he'd just stay under his bed until college.

He was allowed to entertain this delusion for about twelve hours.

The next morning, he awoke to his mother knocking on his door. "Max," she called. "Wake up. You have a visitor!"

A few minutes later, Max was downstairs to find Molly

sitting in his living room, wearing a baseball cap and look-ing impatient.

"Come on," she said. "You're going to be late for practice!"

Max shook his head. "Molly, I told you, I don't—"

Her eyes got big. She seemed to be trying to tell him something, and Max wished desperately he spoke girl. "Yes," she said, voice full of portent. "You do."

He nodded. Like he could ever say no to Molly.

Max's mom smiled. "Honey, are you playing *baseball*?"

"That's right!" Molly said. "He tried to get out of it, but we thought he might have natural gifts."

Max stopped. Had Molly hit those last words a little too hard? His mom seemed to be looking at her a little strangely, but just then turned and gave Max a smile. A few minutes later he was wearing sweats and sitting in the backseat of the Kinsman family's SUV, Molly next to him.

"Molly, what—"

"Shhhh," she whispered, pointing to her father, who was driving. "We're not going to practice. Look!"

She held out a flyer. Max looked at it. And everything inside of him turned to goo. There were a lot of words, but only three stood out to him:

MEET BEAU FLETCHER

Max gagged.

"Can you believe it?" Molly whispered. "It's a charity thing. My dad got tickets as an early birthday present. You get to get his autograph and everything!" She produced a baseball from her bag and held it out like an apple.

"Uh-huh," Max said, very very very faintly.

"So, I think you should just tell him! Walk up to him and tell him who you are!" She looked at him expectantly. "You can do that, right?"

"Molly, I—I don't know."

Her eyes narrowed. "Max, come on. He's a world-famous baseball player! He must have a kazillion dollars. He should be taking care of you and your mom! I mean, if he's your *dad* . . . "

"Molly," he said, though his throat was closing in, "I-I can't do that."

"Why not?"

Max opened his mouth and closed it like a goldfish.

"Yes, you can, Max. I know you don't like to make trouble. But if not for you, then for your mom! Anyway, don't you think he'd want to know about you? His son? Isn't that fair to him? Give him a chance to *do the right thing.*"

Mouth opened. Mouth closed. And again.

"And if you don't want to tell him," she said, "I will . . .

unless you can give me a good reason not to."

Silence settled in the car then, thick like eternity.

"No," said Max, voice like a strangled squirrel's. Molly raised her eyebrows. Open. Close. Open. Close. "I'll do it," he said finally.

There was no way out of this, that was clear. She would hate him if she knew the truth. He would be a laughingstock. He would spend the rest of the year hanging by his underwear from the flagpole. Max had made his bed, now he'd have to strangle himself with the sheets. He turned and looked out of the window.

At best, Fletcher would just think Max was crazy. He would sign his baseball, wonder at this boy's obvious brain damage. And move on.

And at worst, at worst, well—

Max closed his eyes for the rest of the car ride.

Molly's father dropped them off at a hotel, and they walked in slowly. Molly was practically buzzing. Max felt like toxic sludge. His intestines kept looping in on themselves. She led him through the lobby into a big ballroom and to their place in line.

"You want to do this, right?" she asked as they got in line.

Max nodded weakly. The line might have taken six

minutes or six days, Max wasn't sure. Whatever it was, it wasn't long enough, and soon Max and Molly were next in line to see the white-toothed, curly-haired, iron-jawed, big-eared pride of New Hartford, New York. Max had seen Beau Fletcher so many times on TV and on billboards and in the eyes of kids around him who thought maybe they could be great someday, too. And he'd always seemed like he only existed in two dimensions. But here Beau Fletcher was, a person. A very very large person, but a person nonetheless.

"You go first," he said to Molly.

Molly nodded. "Second thoughts?" she whispered.

"No," he said. "No. Definitely not." After all, he told himself, she had a point. If Beau Fletcher had in fact been his dad, telling him would be the right thing to do. Definitely.

And then the usher urged her forward. And as soon as she was in front of Beau, her eyes lit up and a shy smile appeared on her face. "Hi," Molly breathed to Beau. "You're, like, my hero."

And judging by the expression on her face, Max knew it was true. He was lucky his dad wasn't some utility infielder.

Fletcher gave her a smile. "I'm flattered. You are . . . ?"

"Molly," she said, handing him a baseball. "To Molly."

It must be something, Max thought, seeing the excitement flash in Molly's eyes, to make people feel like this. Like they mattered.

"Any message?" Fletcher asked.

"Um, Strike 'em out?"

"You play softball, huh?"

Molly straightened. "No. Baseball."

"Baseball!" Fletcher laughed, and flashed Molly a smile full of charm. "Do you throw like a girl?"

Molly blinked and took the baseball back. She stood there for a moment, staring at Fletcher. Something passed over her face. Then she turned to Max. "Batter up," she said, her expression inert.

And that was it. There was no waiting anymore. Max stepped forward.

"Hello." Beau Fletcher looked up at him with an automatic smile. He really was a large large man. He could probably crush Max with one arm. But he wouldn't. Beau was a good guy, Max could see that now. Just because he was the greatest baseball player in the world didn't automatically make him a jerk. "Um," Fletcher said, and Max realized he was staring dumbly again. "Do you want me to sign something?"

Max thrust the baseball in his general direction. Beau

Fletcher poised his pen, and in two blinks, the ball was signed in thick black ink. Molly poked Max in the ribs. "Do it," she hissed.

"Um, Mr. Fletcher," gasped Max. Beau glanced up at him. ". . . I, um . . . I'm your son."

Behind him, Molly exhaled. Beau Fletcher sat slowly back in his chair.

"Excuse me?"

"I'm your son. Um. You don't know about me, but—my mom—um . . ."

Fletcher drew back and eyed Max for a moment. His eyes narrowed. "Look, kid," he said, leaning in, "I'm pretty sure that's not true." He articulated each word carefully.

Max tried to speak the truth with his eyes. *I know. I know. But play along, okay? Please?* Beau Fletcher was a good man, the kind of man who inspired people, who made them feel like they mattered. This sort of thing happened with kids and professional baseball players all the time. They had a connection. The baseball player looked the kid in the eye and saw the wish in his heart—hit a home run for me, come visit me in the hospital, pretend to be my dad. . . .

Beau Fletcher did look Max in the eye. And he leaned in. And Max leaned in, too, because he could do nothing else.

Beau said something to Max in a low voice, and it took Max a minute to process the words, because Beau was not playing along. Beau said something baseball players are never, ever supposed to say to kids.

Max stared. Tears burned his eyes. And then Molly pushed next to him. "What did you just say to him?" she spat.

"Are you in on this, too?" Fletcher said.

"I used to look up to you," Molly said. "You were my hero."

Fletcher stood up a little. "I don't know who put you kids up to this." Behind them, people began to murmur. And Max, Max could not move at all.

"What's wrong with you?" Molly continued. "You're on commercials for *milk*! And you're nothing but a jerk!" She pounded on the table.

"Hey"—Fletcher looked around—"keep it down."

Yeah, Max thought. *Keep it—*

"This is your *son*!" she proclaimed.

Silence, all around. And stares, from every direction. The usher stood dumbly, as if none of his usher training had prepared him for this.

Molly straightened and looked around. "That's right," she said to the crowd loudly. "This is his son, Maximilian

Funk from New Hartford, NY. His mom raised him all by herself. And Beau Fletcher won't even acknowledge him."

And then two security guards appeared next to them and grabbed both their arms. And then they were being hauled out of the room. Max caught one last glance at Beau Fletcher, who was watching them go.

Then they were outside of the hotel; the security guards yelled at them for a while. Molly's big green eyes looked so confused, and Max wanted to help her, protect her; but he could not because this was all his fault.

And then they were alone, and silence settled around them like dust. And tears rolled down Max's cheeks. And he turned to Molly and began to speak.

"Molly, Molly, look. I'm sorry. I can't take it anymore. I lied. I lied about the whole thing. I just wanted to impress you. I wanted you to like me. It got out of hand. I'm so sorry. You're so tough and brave and amazing and—"

He couldn't go on. Molly was staring at him coolly. Her Catwoman eyes looked suddenly as if they might be capable of terrible things.

"I'm so sorry," he said again.

And then one corner of Molly's mouth drew up. "Oh, Max," she said, her voice suddenly feline. "I knew you were lying the whole time."

"Wha—?"

"It's the stupidest story I've ever heard."

"Then what . . . ?"

"Because you expected me to believe it. I wanted to see how far you'd go. How stupid you thought I really was. Turns out pretty stupid. Why, because I'm a girl? Or because I'm good at baseball? Or both?"

"No, I—"

She tossed her red hair, and it looked like fire. "You're just like everyone else. All you care about is being cool. Nobody cares what a person's really like."

"No, no, that's not—"

"And besides"—Molly took a step closer. She stared him down. Max could not move—"now you'll never ever say you throw like a girl again." Her eyes narrowed. She leaned in and hissed, "You *wish* you threw like a girl."

Max stared. His mouth hung open. Molly seemed six feet tall all of a sudden, and her eyes took your secrets from you. And Max felt what it was like to step into the batter's box and see her staring at you, to look into those eyes as she probed you for your weaknesses. And he knew without a doubt that he, like every sixth grader in the city who would face her that season, had just struck out.

AGAINST ALL ODDS
BY DUSTIN BROWN

Dustin Brown plays right wing for the Los Angeles Kings of the National Hockey League. He is also the Kings' captain. Dustin was named captain at the age of twenty-three, becoming the youngest captain—and the only American-born captain—in the history of the Kings' franchise. Dustin has also played for Team USA in the World Championships four times. He was a 2009 NHL All-Star and served as an alternate captain of the silver medal–winning United States Olympic Team for the 2010 Vancouver Winter Olympics.

Drafted thirteenth in the first round of the 2003 NHL draft, Dustin grew up in Ithaca, New York, where he started playing hockey at age three. From the moment he started playing, it was clear he had skill on the ice—but so did lots of other kids. What made him so great that he was able to *become the All-Star captain of an NHL team? Talent plays a huge part in his story. So does determination and commitment, by him and by his parents, who backed him up every step of the way.*

Here is his story . . . so far.

YOUTH HOCKEY (1987–1999)
ITHACA YOUTH HOCKEY ASSOCIATION

More than 350,000 kids (boys and girls) play hockey each year as part of USA Hockey, the system in charge of amateur hockey in the United States. From 1987–1999, Dustin was among them.

When I Was Really Little . . .

I started playing hockey when I was three years old because my big brother Brendan was playing, and I wanted to do everything he did. I learned by pushing a chair around on the ice. Funny enough, my dad can't even skate. It was just a result of the fact that my brother played hockey, and I wanted to do everything that he got to do.

My early years as a hockey player were probably a lot like everyone else's. Though I guess I was maybe a little bit crazier about the game than the other kids. Once I got into it, it became my favorite thing to do in the world. That's been true from the time I started playing, even to this day.

I believe I started playing organized hockey around age five or six, which is the Tykes level. The one thing I remember—and it's a vivid memory; I have a photo—is my very first hockey jersey. It was green and white, and I had all red equipment, so I basically looked like a Christmas decoration. I remember the jersey because my father's restaurant sponsored my team, which was Bryan's Landing; the logo was an open-cockpit two-seater plane. I also remember it so well because my grandfather was there to watch me, which I believe was the last time he saw me skate. The other thing I remember was how thin the jersey was. It was a meshlike material. Pretty cheap stuff. The reason I remember that is because I played on an outdoor rink and the jersey wasn't like the ones I wear now, which are nice and thick. This jersey was thin . . . very thin . . . which means I was freezing.

As cold as I was, though, it didn't matter to me. I always had a ball on the ice.

Squirt and Peewee (Ages 9–12)

When I was between nine and ten, I was a Squirt. Then I was a Peewee when I was eleven and twelve. I've got some great memories of those years. The Squirts and Peewees were each divided into two levels in my town. One level was called Travel, which was the more or less "elite" team. The other was called Snowbelt. Both teams got to travel, but the Travel team was on the road a lot more, going a lot farther away and playing against tougher competition.

You had to try out for the Travel team. I did, and I made it. My dad and I began to hit the road, and it seemed like that was what we did every weekend for years.

Once I got to be on a Travel team, things got a little more serious. I couldn't skip practices or games. If I wanted to play any other sports, I had to fit them in around my hockey schedule. I worked hard on my schoolwork, and I never needed to be told to do it. Ever since I was a little kid going to tournaments on the weekends, I could get most of my work done in the car or on the way to the hockey game. So once I was there, I could kind of have fun.

The trips were fantastic. Since I was always with the same group of kids, it was like we were hanging out in our fort. I loved the hockey, but I think my best memories were off the ice, playing minihockey in the hallways and then running from the security guards.

We really traveled a lot. We usually left Thursday night or Friday morning, depending on how far away the games were. We would have two games on Friday, two games on

Saturday. If you were on one of the better teams and play-ing in the semifinals and finals, you'd have two games on Sunday too, so it was pretty busy. But at that age, we could play six games in three days and be fine. We'd play mini-hockey, we'd go out to dinner, and we'd just hang around with one another. I played with the same group of seven or eight kids from the time I was eight until the time I was about fifteen. I really created a bond with those guys.

When I wasn't playing hockey, I played baseball and lacrosse. I always loved hockey, but it was great to have time to play other sports too. Sometimes, today, I think parents push their kids to specialize in one sport. You've got kids that are, like, eight, nine years old who are one-sport athletes, which I don't think is in anyone's best interest. I also liked to read . . . sort of. My favorite books were the Goosebumps books by R. L. Stine. Each book was numbered. I liked col-lecting them, trying to get every single one.

Support System
My dad owned a restaurant in my hometown. It was right by the airport. He worked hard, but now that I look back at it, his main job was just carting me around. He worked Monday through Thursday, and then we would go on our hockey trips.

Even though hockey was expensive, my dad always found a way for me to be able to play. It's not only the cost of the Youth Hockey Association fees, it's also the travel and renting motel rooms.

I remember coming back with him from a game one time. We had an Isuzu Trooper, and I took a picture on the way home because we had just passed two hundred thousand miles on the vehicle. That was pretty cool. A whole lot of those were Travel team miles.

Early Mornings

I love to play hockey. But I don't always love to work out. When I was a kid, I sometimes had to get up at 4:30 in the morning for practice. I can't say I was overly excited about it. I'd be half asleep, but I'd get dressed—everything but my skates—and my dad would put me in the car and we would go. When I was a Peewee, I had two practices a week. One would be Monday morning at 5:30, and the other would be Wednesday afternoon at 5:30. I got used to it over time. I got into a rhythm. Once I was in the rink I was fine and ready to go.

Bantam (Ages 13–14)

Things started to change by the time I got to be a Bantam. For one thing, some of the kids who started out really great found they weren't so great anymore. I played against a kid from a nearby town when we were ten years old. He was like Wayne Gretzky back then. By the time we were fourteen, he wasn't any good at all. What happened? If he was so much better than me when we were ten, how come I'm playing professional hockey and he's not?

Did everyone just catch up to him? Or did he not put in the work? I don't know; but I do know that at age twelve or thirteen, some kids will grow a foot in a year, and others won't grow until they're eighteen. Even at my level, I see guys who, for their first couple of years, don't seem as if they're going to be players and then all of a sudden they figure it out. They get stronger physically, they get bigger, they refine parts of their game they weren't focused on before, and they become great players. It's hard work, and it takes a lot of drive. For most of us, we've been at it our whole lives.

When you're twelve years old, there is a big gap between the really good players and the other players. There's still a gap at the NHL level, but it's a much smaller gap from the worst player to the best player on the ice.

When I was about twelve, thirteen, fourteen, I'd be going to the rink and skating when most kids were probably going and hanging out with their friends. It was something I enjoyed. I played other sports too—I kept on playing baseball until I was thirteen. I played lacrosse most of the way through high school. But it was at this point where I kind of needed to pick one sport if I was going to be serious about it. And hockey was my passion, so I stuck with hockey.

The last year I played in Ithaca, I had my first big disappointment. I tried out for the New York State Select 15—a team of the best fourteen- and fifteen-year-olds in the state. I made the central New York team. But I got cut from the twenty-man statewide team.

It was a surprise. But I learned from it. It's one thing to be the best player in a small town like Ithaca. But then I got dumped into a bigger pond, and there were more fish. I started to realize that there're a lot of really good players out there. At fourteen, I wasn't even in the top twenty players my age in New York. That opened my eyes a bit.

JUNIORS (1999–2003)

Of the 350,000 kids who play Youth Hockey, only 30,000 make the cut to play on an official amateur basis by the time they get to the Junior Hockey level (ages 17–20). Junior Hockey is the step between Youth Hockey and NCAA College Hockey or, in some cases, the NHL. From 1999–2003, Dustin was one of those players, starting with the Syracuse Stars in 1999 and moving up to the Guelph Storm of the Ontario Hockey League (OHL) in 2000.

I was upset when I got cut from the Select 15 when I was fourteen. But things got better the next year when I joined the Syracuse Stars. They are a Tier III Junior team—Tier I being the most competitive in the country—but the play was still plenty competitive. It was a big jump up for me from Ithaca Youth Hockey.

Some of the guys on the team were far from home and still in high school. So they lived with "billet families"— families who were paid to house and feed Junior Hockey players. I lived close enough to Syracuse that I didn't have to billet out there. I was pretty busy with hockey by then, but I still kept up with stuff at home.

Most of the guys playing on the Stars were older than me. Some of them had finished high school and were playing Juniors hoping for a scholarship from an NCAA Division I college team or maybe even to make it into the NHL draft—though that's kind of a big leap from a Tier III team.

My hockey really improved over that year. Our team won the national championship, and then right after that I made the Select 16s. Within a year, not only did I make the New York team, I was picked as one of the top twenty players in the nation as a sixteen-year-old. That was the first moment when I thought that maybe I could really do this for a living. And that's when I had a really big decision to make.

Canada? Or College?

In 2000, Dustin got the chance to try out for the Guelph Storm of the Ontario Hockey League. This was a big leap and would require him to live with a billet family himself—far from home. That wasn't the only thing that made the decision tough. Leaving the US to play hockey in Canada meant that Dustin would be forfeiting his chance to get a Division I college hockey scholarship. It meant that he was putting college aside—maybe for a while, maybe forever—in the hope of making it to the NHL. Even though about 20 percent of players on active rosters in the NHL come from the OHL, he was banking on some very long odds.

When I got the chance to go to Canada, it was my parents who really helped me figure out what to do. I was only fifteen. My parents were worried about my schooling, because I was giving up my college eligibility going into the OHL.

My dad said, "If you want to do this, they'll give you a school package." He figured the OHL would find a way to help me pay for college somehow. My mom was really worried about me going; she didn't want me to leave home. But at the end of the day, they both said, "If you want to do this, you should do it. You can always go to school after." They were really supportive of my decision, just like they had always been. I had to grow up a bit quicker, but I chose to do it that way.

Though hockey was Dustin's focus during his three years in Ontario, he stuck to the books too. In fact, he was the Ontario Hockey League Scholastic Player of the Year every year he was there, winning their Bobby Smith Trophy three years in a row. He is the only player in that league ever to win the trophy in three consecutive years.

According to the league, the trophy is awarded in honor of former Ottawa 67's star Bobby Smith, and is symbolic of the high standard of excellence that Smith displayed in the classroom as well as on the ice during his outstanding Junior career.

In addition to his high academic average while in Guelph, Dustin also was the highest-scoring player in his last year of high school, scoring 34 goals with 42 assists, good for 76 points.

As Dustin's hockey skills continued to improve, he kept his focus on his goal of making it to the NHL. It's not easy for every NHL hopeful to keep that fire burning.

I was pretty motivated, as I'm sure a lot of other kids out there are. But the main thing was that my dad and my mom were really good about supporting me in my decisions all the time I was growing up. If I wanted to go to a hockey tournament every weekend when I was a kid, it was because I wanted to go—not because my dad pressured me into going.

I played hockey in the winter, and I would sometimes go on my own to the rink and skate during the summertime. But I didn't play on hockey teams all year long when I was a kid. I did other things.

I think I stuck with hockey the whole way through because I was self-motivated.

I wanted to be an NHL player my whole life. But my dad wasn't sitting there saying, "Okay, if I push this kid, he'll make it." It was more like, "Go have fun. If it works out, it works out." I realized that if I wanted to do this, I would have to do it for myself. I was going to have to work really hard at it, be disciplined. Lucky for me, I have always loved to play hockey. Because there are lots of other things that fourteen-, fifteen-, and sixteen-year-old kids want to do. But for me, it was all about going to the rink and playing hockey.

I developed a lot as a player and as a person in Ontario.

I had to learn a lot of responsibility. I was living with a billet family, so I always had food on the table or a ride if I needed it, but it's a little different when it's not your own family. I was away from all my family and friends, and I kind of grew up a little bit quicker.

A Shot at the Big Time: The NHL Draft

Of the thirty thousand players in Junior Hockey each year, about two hundred are invited to the NHL draft at age eighteen. In 2003, Dustin was one of them. Thirty players in his year were selected in the first round of the draft. Dustin was one of them, too—number thirteen. He was drafted by the Los Angeles Kings.

I went from being a little kid in Ithaca to being an NHL player within a matter of three and a half years. It happened very quickly and was a lot to get adjusted to. It was definitely a whirlwind. When I was eighteen, I think I was rated number two in the world. I was selected number thirteen overall in the 2003 draft. It was overwhelming, but at the same time it was something I'd wanted to do since I was five years old.

When I was thirteen, like every kid, I was saying, "Oh, yeah, I'm going play in the NHL." Suddenly, within five years, I was playing in my first NHL game.

Dustin played his first game in the NHL on October 9, 2003, a month before his nineteenth birthday. He got a penalty for high-sticking.

So I was expecting, I was *wanting* to be in that situation. I remember being at the draft, and I had a lot of family and friends there with me, and it was a really exciting time. But the flip side of that was once I was drafted I realized, "Okay, I'm drafted. Now the real hard work starts."

MOVING UP TO THE SHOW (2003)

Of all the hockey players who are selected in the first round of an NHL draft, about eight will make careers as professional hockey players, playing in more than two hundred NHL games. Dustin, who has played in more than five hundred NHL games since 2003, was part of an unusually strong draft year. Of the thirty players drafted with Dustin in the first round, five players went on to lead their teams in scoring in the 2007–2008 season. Ten players have been part of either an All-Star team, the Olympics (for the United States or Canada), or both, including Dustin, who was on both the 2009 All-Star team and the 2010 US Olympic team, for which he was an alternate captain.

Getting drafted is one thing. But many players get drafted and never play a game. On top of that, my draft year was abnormal because we had pretty much an All-Star team out of the first round.

Going from the draft to actually getting a spot on the team takes a lot of hard work, and it depends on your abilities, obviously. But a lot of it is timing. There are a lot of players who got drafted around the same time as me who are still playing in the AHL (North American hockey's minor professional league system) and trying to make it into the NHL. Or else they've given it up. A lot has to do with where you fit on the team. The timing was good for me in Los Angeles.

I tried to establish myself early. I knew I was going to have to find a way to stand out. I wasn't going to score twenty goals a season like I did in the OHL or in Youth Hockey. I needed to find a way to stay in this league and stay with the Kings. So I started to develop the physical side of my game, becoming very aggressive. That filled a void on the team and gave me a spot. As an eighteen-year-old, all you're trying to do is stay on the team. And it kind of became the trademark of my game.

Some sportswriters say Dustin has a lot of "sandpaper" in his game.

Once I was established, it was a matter of continuing to

work hard to get better.

The more you play at this level, the more you learn. My first year, I ran out of position a lot just trying to hit someone. I would make the hit, but it took me out of position for the rest of the play. My game's come a long way since then. An interesting thing about hitting: it's not always size that makes the difference. I've known guys who are smaller than me who can knock me down. I've known guys bigger than me who try to hit me and can't even move me. A lot of it is timing. It's not an easy thing to judge. I make a lot of hits, but I also miss a lot of hits.

CAPTAIN BROWN (2007–PRESENT)

There are thirty teams in the NHL, with more than 750 active players. Each team has a captain. When Dustin was named captain of the Kings in 2007 at age twenty-three, he was both the youngest captain and the first US-born captain in team history.

Becoming captain was an opportunity that developed naturally as my position here with the Kings did. It was something I thought I would be capable of doing, the way the team was being crafted. Everything just kind of lined up right for me. And when the opportunity came, I was excited.

I've been captain for four years now. I still learn a lot

every day. In my first three years on the team, before I was captain, I hardly ever talked at team meetings. Even now that I'm in a leadership role, I still don't talk a lot in a room. I try to lead by example. If I come in and work my tail off, there's no excuse for any other player not to. If a leader leads the way in terms of work ethic, doing extra stuff after practice, stuff like that, it leaves little room for error, especially in a team environment. It's pretty simple: just go out there, do your work, get what you need to do done. It's the same way on the ice—I try to do all the little things right. It's a hockey game, and people make mistakes. But if the intent is there, I think everyone can kind of build on that.

A Dream Job?

It's definitely a job. I don't get paid to play hockey. I get paid to *prepare to be* a hockey player in the summertime, working out. Ask any professional athlete. Playing the game is the fun part. Working out three hours a day in the summer is *not* my favorite part of being a professional hockey player, that's for sure. Once my season is over, I take two, three, four weeks maybe to regenerate. And after that I go to the gym every day. It's not because I *want* to go to the gym. It's because I've *got* to go there. I'm not complaining. Being a professional hockey player is what I've always wanted to do. There's just a lot that goes into it that the average fan maybe doesn't know about.

Dynasty?

I've got three boys, all under the age of four. My oldest two have been out on the ice a little. My oldest one can kind of stand up and push the puck around. My middle one has been out there a couple of times. He's going to take a while to develop because . . . he's two and a half now, and when he runs around, he's like an accident waiting to happen.

But the problem is, I'm not really sure how to teach them. I learned by pushing a chair around, and that's what I'm trying to do with them. But it's really hard to explain hockey and skating. All that stuff came naturally to me, so I don't know how to teach it to my kids. It's actually a very weird dynamic. My dad didn't teach me how to skate. But he didn't know how to skate, so that's okay. I know how to skate, but I can't teach my own kids how to skate! I guess I had my own drive, my own passion. I don't know if there's any way to communicate that to someone else.

At the End of the Day . . .

People ask me what it's like to come home after a game, what I do to settle myself down. There are good days and bad days. The older I've gotten, the more tame I've become, especially now that I have a family. Before, I'd be working on my game all the time: in the gym and at the rink. If things weren't going well at the rink, they weren't going well in life, period. That was my life. Now that I have a family I've changed my perspective. Obviously, I'm still working hard and trying to do my best on the ice. But when I get home from the rink, I realize there are things that are more important than winning or losing a game. At the end of the day, my family is why I play the game.

THE DISTANCE
BY JACQUELINE WOODSON

Coach calls me over after the half-mile relay. Head between my legs, heart still on fire, trying hard to catch even a tiny breath. I'll take that—a tiny breath. Just a little airflow back into my lungs. Just enough to stop the burning. Maybe a little bit more could make its way down to my legs, keep them from trembling.

Laurence jogs up to me with some of the other guys. "You blew the third leg, Cash," he says. "Your race sucked a big one."

Even with my hard breathing and bent-overness, I just give him a look and he steps off. A little.

"He's gonna make you do it again. The 800's your new race, man. Might as well get up and start breathing."

"That's the last time I'm running it. Ever," I say. All of them look blurry and far away. I see the fourth leg, Jason, looking down on me like he can't believe I'm human. Like he's wondering why I'm even alive.

"I could have caught them if you would've kicked a little," Jason says. "You rigged instead of kicking. You, like, just stopped. Who just stops like that?"

"I didn't stop!" But the words come too quick, and it hurts my chest to shoot them out like that.

"It's Penn Relays, Cash! You just blew up Penn Relays. You just blew it for all of us."

"We suck anyway," I say. But the words come out weak and broken up. *I hate relays,* I want to say. *They suck.* But that would make me not a *team person.* That would mean I sucked for even thinking it. Then all of them are jogging off again, warming up for their other races.

In the race that got us here, I ran relaxed and easy—like Coach said to. Didn't break two minutes but Coach said it was a good beginning. The others hustled and we got our qualifying time. "When we get there," Coach had said to me, "you're gonna run it different. Harder. Faster. You're made for the half mile. Want it. Just want it."

I don't. This kinda pain isn't something anybody could want.

"Cashew!" Coach calls again.

I put up my hand, trying to show him I'm half dead, can't answer, can't even say for the hundredth millionth time *That's not my name.*

It's Cashay. Calvin James "CJ" *Cashay.* It's actually Cashay-Brunner, but by the time I hit fifth grade, the Brunner and the CJ were gone, and I was just Cashay. By the time I started running, Cashay was gone, too.

I take another deep breath, try to stand. But my side is on fire, so I grab it and bend over again. There's the urban legend about the kid who drank soda, ate some kind of crackling, popping candy, then ran a race and died at the finish line but not before he ran the fastest race of his life, leaving everybody else in the dust.

"What happened to you, Cashay? How'd you get beat down like that? How'd you lose so . . . so *badly*? That's not you."

Coach is above me now, so close he doesn't even have to raise his voice to talk to me. So he doesn't—he's whispering.

"I'm just curious. Truly, truly curious."

I didn't drink the soda and eat the popping candy, I want to say. *So now I'm just dying.*

I close my mouth and try to get some air in through my nose. I'm staring at his legs: brown and still real muscular.

He's wearing blue-and-gray running shorts—school colors—and his legs go on and on. He ran the last leg on the quarter-mile relay in college a million years ago *and* quarter-mile hurdles, Olympic trials—close enough to *almost* taste Atlanta in 1996—everything. He's still the real deal and tries not to let the team forget that.

"I don't like relays," I manage to get out—mostly wind but some words too. "I told you I couldn't do it!"

"You told me you didn't want to do it. Not that you couldn't. You died because you didn't want to. You just stopped. It looked like something slammed into you—"

"I hit a wall!"

"You stopped. Your brain. Your mind. Your body. Just stopped."

"Aren't coaches . . . supposed . . . to say stuff like . . ." I take another deep breath, enough air to get some more words out. "Like . . . you did . . . your best? I'm proud of you. . . . Good race."

"It wasn't a good race, and I'm not proud of you. You're confusing me with a parent. They have to say that kind of crap. You looked really jacked up at the 600. At the 7, you looked like— You looked really bad, man. You just looked *bad*, Cashew. . . ."

After another moment, I try to stand up straight, hold

on to my back with my hands, and take more deep breaths as I start walking slow around the outside of the track. Coach follows me, then pulls my arm and starts jogging real slow just a little bit ahead. I shake my arm free and try to keep up with him. The last thing I want is for people to see Coach holding me up.

"I got this," I tell him.

"Not bad ugly—that's not what I'm saying," Coach continues, still real quietly. "Bad like you could care less. That kinda bad. I could see it on your face from across the field."

I don't say anything, just keep jogging beside him.

"Your legs are a mile long. You don't have one single ounce of extra weight anywhere. . . ."

Air is finally making its way to my lungs again. But I keep my head and arms down as I run—*lopey like a fawn,* Coach says. *Real relaxed. That's good.* We jog for about a hundred yards without saying anything. Then he starts again. "How did you manage to get lapped in an 800, Cashew? You have to be running backward to get lapped in that race."

"Rigged." I take another deep breath. "The wall hit me. That back straightaway's got a wind to it. And that guy from Packer's on steroids. Look at him. No other sixth grader's got a beard. He looks like he's fifty, no offense."

"I'm thirty-three, and he DESTROYED you!"

"I don't like relays, okay!" I stop jogging and look right at him. "I'm an only child, remember? I'm used to doing things alone."

"You stop being an only child when you step onto the track on *my* team, Cash. Your *only* ended there."

"I like running just my races—

"Your races are everybody's races. You know how this works. Points are points. Relay points. Individual points. It all adds up. So don't give me that 'my own race' junk. None of these races belong to you." He starts jogging again, and I do too. Not because I feel like jogging next to him. I just don't want to look stupid on the field. Again.

Coach isn't mean. Not even a little bit. His command of the English language just kinda sucks when he's mad. Even if he was born here in New York. And his parents too. And their parents, he told us. He said, "Bootstrap American to the bone." Then he gave us this real long look. "It means something," he said. "To work your butt off and try to *do* something. Try to *change* something."

"This race sucks," I say to him, trying to shake that lecture from my head. Maybe it was a month ago, but it's the one that keeps crawling back to haunt me. *Try to change something.*

"I don't even know why you put me in it, Coach. It's not for humans. I'm a quarter-miler."

"And in the open races, you run an amazing quarter mile. In the open races, you fly. But not on the relays. We both know, on the quarter-mile relay, we got four guys who bust up your time. That's why I thought I'd give you a chance in the 800."

"We made the qualifying time," I say real slow. "We got here."

I see something move across Coach's face. Like a sadness and a rage all at once. Then, real quick, it's gone. He shakes his head like he's trying to shake whatever's in it out again.

"Yeah, Cash. We qualified. We got here. We ran Penn Relays. Maybe that's enough for you." He looks at me. "Maybe for you, that's always going to be okay."

He keeps looking at me like he's waiting for me to answer.

"I did everything you said, Coach: relaxed on the curve, tried to get some speed on that back straightaway—everything." .

The stadium is packed. At the 300, there's a photographer taking every runner's picture just before they cross the finish line. Me and Coach jog past the javelin throwers, and I try to lift my shoulders a little. Buff up. Any one of them could be two of me. Probably steroids. The whole world looks like it's on steroids. The whole world is shorter and stronger than me. My moms both swear that one day I'm gonna love every bit about the way I look. Both of them have that strange ability to lie without twitching or blinking or looking away.

Me and Coach are almost done with our second lap around when he says, real quiet, "You did, Cashew. You did everything I said. But you didn't push yourself. You didn't run like running was all you had. Just for the two minutes it takes to run that race. Inside that race, running is everything. Running is all there is. And after you win, the world comes back—and it's different." Coach stops talking and looks at me. "There's not a thing about you that says you can't blow everyone on this track away, Cashew. But for some reason, you're deciding to be regular. . . . You don't have to be regular."

"It's *their* race, Coach! It's not mine. Let them *win* it. I'm not giving them this, too. Let them get some bootstraps!"

Coach looks at me again. He almost smiles, but he doesn't. Instead he kicks out his leg and starts sprinting, fast. I lean forward and start running hard to keep up with him. We do a hundred-yard dash, then jog a few steps and break into another one, me right at Coach's heels even though he's running full-out. Maybe people are watching. People tell us we run alike: all leg, upper body loose, hands open. But at the end of our sprints, Coach isn't even breathing hard. My chest is on fire.

"Just like that," Coach says. "They'll keep on running long after you've stopped. Whether you win the damn race or not, Cash. You disappear. They go off and shine. And you won't be able to blame them, cuz you made the choice to fade away. You're better than that. You're faster and smarter than that."

Then he drops me with the rest of the team and the assistant coaches in the warm-up area. Some of the guys are stretching. Others are doing practice dashes, running out fifty yards, then jogging back. Nobody says anything to me, and I sit off to the side, start stretching my hamstrings that are already crazy-tight.

The day Coach gave us that bootstraps lecture, Laurence was the only one to say something back to him.

"I don't need straps, Coach," Laurence said. "I'm golden. Don't need to change anything. You never heard of a silver spoon? My dads said if I never want to work—ever—then I don't have to." Laurence looked around at all of us. "Don't even have to shine my spoon!" Some kids laughed. I wasn't one of them. "And I'm not planning on working, cuz working sucks! Getting up early . . ."

A bunch of guys agreed with him. I kept my mouth closed. We were in the locker room, and it was hot and wet smelling. Smelled like armpits and all those funky body parts that explode with stink the minute a piece of clothing is removed from them.

"Then why're you running, Laurence?" Coach asked.

"To get girls. You know how we do." He dapped a couple of the guys, nodding and smiling. But there was a look on his face. Something deep. Something trying to hide.

Coach stopped talking then. Just shook his head. Told us to get dressed, that we were done for the day.

When I got outside that day, it was cold. Sneak-up, late-October cold. Ma was parked out front, the music turned up loud inside the car. Some old guy—Dan Fogelberg or Barry White, I don't remember. They all sounded alike to me: sad and sorry over something they lost—horses, women, card games, stuff like that. I could think of a million things to write songs about besides horses and women and card games.

"Am I going to have to work, Ma? Or is there some silver spoon waiting for me somewhere? Like Laurence has?"

Ma turned the music down and looked at me. Our car

was old. There were some cracks in the leather seats, and the carpet on the floor of it was worn away in some places. Since I was a baby, we'd lived in the same place: a small apartment on the top floor of a brownstone. We owned the apartment, and Moms was always calling it "your inheritance." I stared out the car window, waiting for Ma to answer.

"Your mom and I are always gonna make sure you have what you need, CJ. But, yeah, you'll work . . . of course you'll work."

"But a lot of kids at my school don't have to. . . ."

"And a lot will have to. And that's the great thing and the messed-up thing about living in the USA." Ma smiled at me. Maybe she was trying to make a joke, but I didn't get it. All I was getting was the way things were kinda jacked up in the world. I'd be working my butt off, and Laurence would be sitting in a comfy chair playing games on his phone.

"Doesn't suck if you love what you do, CJ," Ma said. She ran her hand over my head, then turned on the car and started driving.

"It sucks if you have to do it, though."

Ma took a deep breath. She looked like she was about to say something but then she didn't. I leaned my head against the cold window and didn't say anything else for the ride home, thinking the whole way, *It sucks to be me.*

Laurence and the rest of the quarter-mile relay team are getting ready to run. Laurence is bent over, his ankles crossed, his fingertips touching the ground. I should be doing the same thing: stretching out my hamstrings some more.

"Can't believe you let a Packy lap you like that, bro. Two steps with those long legs, and you're around the track."

"Can't believe you blew up our team like that," the second-leg guy says. He hands Laurence the baton and Laurence gets behind him, and the third and fourth legs line up in front so that it goes first leg to fourth leg—back to front. They stand, bent forward now, only a little distance between them, and start running in place.

"Stick!" Laurence says, and the second-leg guy reaches his hand back so that Laurence can slap the baton into it. They go through the line doing this a few times, their motions fluid as water—like they've been doing this all their lives. Like it's natural as breathing.

"He didn't lap me. What was my split?"

"You don't want to know your splits, trust me." Laurence says between passes.

"It's a stupid race," I say. "I don't know why he even put

me in it. It's not for human beings. It's for people on steroids like that Packy dude."

A whole bunch of Packer guys are still jumping all over the steroids guy. He's grinning wide and scratching his beard.

Laurence and the others finish their practice and go back to stretching.

"The truth is, you got lapped because you ran it like a quarter mile. That's why you died at the 600. Your first split was 57." Laurence doesn't even look up from his stretch. He's in eighth grade, and for some reason, he's always all coolness. Like he's got everything covered forever and ever, amen.

"I ran a 57 quarter? That's my best time! That's like world-record material right there—" The air and strength is all back in me now, and I do some happy-dancing, not caring who's watching.

"Your second split was a sweet 1:37. Which means you ran your second quarter at 97, which might break this meet's record for the slowest quarter mile ever run."

I stop dancing real fast. 1:37 isn't good. It's old person with a cane, one leg, and a swollen foot time.

"That's what killed us Second Leg—Joseph—says. That's what buried us."

"It's not two quarter miles." Laurence unfolds himself

and finally looks at me. He's not as tall as me, but he's got muscles already. He's wearing a headband, cuz otherwise his hair would be in his eyes. The band is school colors, and anybody else might get all kinds of words thrown at them for wearing it.

"When you run it again, remember that."

The first call for their race comes, and the four of them jog over. Me and Laurence have the two-mom thing in common, but that's about where it ends. Laurence has two dads too. And all his parents live in the same building together. To top it all off, he's the only child. He can keep his silver spoon, because having all those people in my ear all the time would make me crazy.

The first legs of the relay are down in the starts, fixing their fingers, getting their butts in the air. Ready. Laurence is on the inside, his favorite spot. The caller yells, "Set!" and the runners lift their butts higher. Then the gun goes off, and they all start running, Laurence taking a fast start and getting about twenty yards ahead of everybody else. He's smiling. I jog slow around the outside of the track, watching them. Laurence slows down a little. I can hear the coach yelling for him to get his arms up. A tall kid from St. Ann's gets close to him, and Laurence sprints out farther. The crowd is cheering. By the 200 mark, Laurence is ahead of everyone. I've never seen him run with this kind of distance.

Both my moms are in the stands. Behind them, all four of Laurence's parents are standing up and cheering. Mama is sneak-emailing. I can tell, because her head is down and she has her reading glasses on. Moms is smiling and waving at me. Who knows how long she's been trying to get my attention. I give a quick wave and start pulling my sweats on.

Laurence is still way out ahead of everyone—his face dark, his arms flashing. He's kicked into something new, something fast and strong. Something crazily determined. I looked up at the stands again. His parents are losing it. They only see their son killing the others. They only see him winning. But I see something else. Standing there, my pants half on, my mouth maybe hanging open, I see that Laurence is already running fast toward the second leg and fast away from them. Fast and far away from them. I see him going and going and know right then that he'll keep running until he can't run anymore, until he can look behind himself and not see all that love, all that scream-ing and attention. Not see all those silver spoons getting shoved down his throat. He passes the stick to Joseph with so much distance between him and the second-place team that even Coach is stunned and smiling.

Ma looks up from her email, blows me a kiss. Moms shrugs—a "next time you'll do better" shrug. A "no worries, there'll be another chance" shrug. I smile, nodding. Knowing I will. The desire to run it different is already building. The chance to work crazy-hard at not being regular, at not disappearing. Behind my parents, Laurence's people are cheering.

I see Coach give Laurence the thumbs-up. I see Laurence throw his fist in the air. I feel the hard "Yeah!" he's screaming blowing toward me. I want to say, "Keep on running, Laurence. You got this."

But instead I just watch him—thinking about next week's 800. I'm gonna run it harder next week. Different. Better.

And maybe after next week, I'll run it for years and years. Hard and fast and way beyond regular. Like I'm running *to* something . . . like the running's all I have.

Coach looks over at me, looks hard like he's trying to figure me out, like he can already see the amazing runner I'm gonna be, the records I'm gonna break, the trophies and medals and money . . . Olympic trials and beyond . . .

"Why are you standing there with your mouth hanging open, Cashew?! Move the body! Move. The. Body!! Jeez!"

Or maybe not.

THE MEAT GRINDER
BY CHRIS CRUTCHER

I count from the front of the line back to me. Four. Then I count four down from the front of the line across from me. Rich Saxon. Thirty-five pounds heavier, a full second faster in the forty. The *forty*. Probably an hour faster in the hundred. I run a hundred yards in about the time it takes to get a haircut. If you're third in line.

Saxon is All-Conference.

I'm All-Mack, my family name. But I'm second-string All-Mack and I'm an only child.

I live in Sherman, Idaho. Population 867. Elevation 5,281. One foot over a mile high. In its heyday, Sherman was a booming logging town, but someone forgot to tell the logging companies that when they cut down a tree, they should probably plant one, trees being finite and all. The trees around Sherman eventually went the way of the buffalo on America's Great Plains. Where it once appeared the supply was inexhaustible, the supply is now exhausted, has been for twenty years.

The town fathers, and mothers, have reinvented Sherman in the past three decades. It is not an invention you would grant a patent. Government money in the late 1980s allowed most merchants to renew their storefronts with an Austrian alpine look, investors from Boise and in some cases from as far north as Lewiston put money into a small ski resort and nine-hole golf course, and the nearby South Fork of the Salmon River provided great rapids when the spring runoff turned it downright adventurous. But Sherman is three and a half hours from the nearest accessible airport and our public relations machine runs on maybe two cylinders. The superhighway running in and out of this bustling burg is a winding two lane that requires four-wheel to navigate for most of the winter, so our dreams of turning into a winter sports mecca turned out to be exactly that. To put it bluntly, Sherman, Idaho, is not Sun Valley. What was for one shining season a three-lift ski resort with attending warm mud baths is now a single–rope tow hill open only on the weekends Ross Conner decides to drag himself out of his toasty cabin to crank up the converted lawn-mower engine that powers it. The golf course now serves as a four-wheeler course in summer and a cross-country/snowmobile/dog-racing course in the winter. It's great fun for the locals and no waiting.

The nearest movie theater is almost three hours away; the nearest bowling alley, forty-five minutes. Mayor Probst likes to say, "You can throw down your bedroll in the middle of Main Street at six o'clock at night and not worry about anybody runnin' you over till the snowplows crank up at six the next morning."

Apparently Mayor Probst thinks that's a plus.

That's probably why Mayor Probst is mayor.

The point is, there is nothing to do in Sherman, Idaho, after Labor Day.

Except football.

A guy doesn't have to be a stellar athlete to play football for the Sherman Huskies. Coach Bull Shuster administers the preseason physical with a mirror. He places it under your nose and if you fog it up, you can play. In fact, you kind of have to. If you fail to show on the first day of football practice your freshman year, they come get you. And your parents let them in. It's better to get beat up *with* pads than without.

Which brings me to the peril I now face.

We call this drill the "meat grinder." Two lines face each other, maybe five feet apart. Coach slaps the football into the gut of the player on the end of one line and the guy up on the far end of the other line is supposed to take him down. Full speed; escape route blocked by your teammates. It's a tackling drill, so I've got to hit Rich Saxon as hard as I can.

If you're a betting man, bet against me.

If you're a life-insurance man, see me before Coach hands Rich the ball.

There are two kinds of guys on this team as I see it: those who want to be here and those who would like to be *any-where* else. When I say anywhere else, I include Hell. Anywhere else is not an option. Sherman, Idaho, as I said, has 867 people. You can run, but you can't hide.

You think they'd be *grateful* you showed up. I'm five-six, a hundred twenty-seven pounds. I have the muscle definition of a chalk outline. My push-up record has yet to reach double digits; my next chin-up will be my first. This is a *sacrifice*. My *thing* is my brain. I'm smart. I get good grades. I love to write. Someday I want to live in a place, far away from my family, where if you threw down your bedroll in the middle of Main Street at six o'clock at night, you'd be squashed by 6:01. My brain is supposed to take me to that place.

And I'm about to serve it up to Rich Saxon.

The good news is I get hit in the head a lot already so this won't be a new experience. My father is a *fan* of child abuse. He doesn't even call it something else, like "discipline" or whatever. "I believe in child abuse." He says that. He says it because his editing function got knocked out of him by *his* dad, who I guess held tight to that very same belief system. Child Protective Services got called on me for the second time in grade school after I showed up with unexplained bruises on my face and neck. Not *totally* unexplained. I gave my teacher the story Hector and Carline told me to give them. Hector and Carline are my mom and dad but they haven't exactly earned the title, so: Hector and Carline. Anyway, the principal called them to school, where he introduced them to our one county social worker who didn't buy that our family dog jumped against me from behind, knocking me into the kitchen sink. She didn't buy it because when she asked the dog's name my dad said Rover, my mother said Fido, and I said Blake. All at the same time. That's how smart my parents are.

My parents are Rover and Fido smart.

So we went to this therapy group filled with *other* people who thought whacking their kids into being good citizens was one of the original eleven amendments to the constitution. The counselor and group leader, Seymour Kraft, pressed upon us that the truth would set us free, that we should all, kids and adults alike, lay it out in its rawest form to the rest of the group. We were sworn to confidentiality, as was Seymour Kraft, so there was no danger of anyone outside the group becoming privy to our secrets.

That's according to Seymour Kraft.

Seymour traveled to Sherman once a week from Boise and didn't get that our county is the largest in the state, area-wise, and the smallest population-wise. We've got about nine thousand people, and maybe twenty last names. You could walk around this county for three days and not run into one person you don't know. To paraphrase a well-known paradox, if you fart in the forest and there's nobody there to hear it, it's on the front page of the county newspaper on Friday.

And like I said, my dad has no editing function. We lasted three sessions before every other person in the group, kids included, returned telling Seymour that Hector Mack had squealed every word spoken in confidentiality to the entire county.

My family was expelled from a *child abuse* group.

The social worker informed Mom that either Dad had to move out of the home until he could complete anger-management classes, or I'd be placed in foster care. I voted for foster care, but it was two to one and Dad took up residence above the Chief Café, where he immediately started an extramarital affair with Rosie Swatch, who also doesn't have an editing function. Carline Mack, who is *way* tougher and meaner than Hector, battered my head because it was my fault he had to leave ("Blake? You little moron. No dog is named Blake."), but she did it from the back so you couldn't see the bruises. She learned that in the child abuse group. Social services was footing the bill for the room above the Chief, so Hector held on to that, then snuck down the back alley around midnight every night to live with us. Rosie Swatch stayed in the room, unbeknownst to my mother, "to make sure no hotel robbers ripped off his stuff." Hector didn't have a pair of underwear at the Chief. His "stuff" was Rosie. So I got whacked on the head by both Hector and Carline. Carline hit me because if Hector had never moved out (my fault) he wouldn't have fallen under the spell of the temptress Rosie Swatch, and Hector hit me because he was afraid to hit Carline.

Might I just say here that if you're tempted by the likes

of Rosie Swatch, you have a bigger problem than simply a missing editing function. Rosie Swatch weighs a pound more than a Buick. And she bathes about as often as my cousin Reggie runs his own Buick through the car wash. Before she started Weight Watchers her steady boyfriend was Smoky Yardley, Sherman's most eligible, least desirable bachelor. When she brought her dress size down to XXXXL, she dropped Smoky like a hot rock and picked up the next-least desirable guy, Hector Mack.

You may be thinking, if you've stayed with my story this far, this Devin Mack kid is a bit politically incorrect, that you shouldn't pay attention to his offensive drivel because he's got no sense of appropriateness. Well, tell you what. I'm nobody around here—around my house, around school, around town. Want to point out someone's Walmart shoes for ridicule? Devin Mack. Want to stuff somebody into a wastebasket and hoist him on top of the lockers? DM's your guy. Wanna trick someone into looking like a giant butt head in front of the coolest girl in school? Mack, Mack, he's our man. . . .

But fear not, Devin Mack, we have an antibullying policy here at Sherman High. We have signs that read BULLY inside a red circle with a slash. Who would *dare* defy such a thing? We have antibullying T-shirts, baseball caps, bumper stickers, backpacks, coffee mugs, drink containers. We have a new character word of the month, *every month*. (We used to have one a week, but I guess the English language is short on character words.)

We had an antibullying bake sale.

Sherman High School is against bullying.

Right.

You can bully me with a *look*. If you're a girl you can bully me by smiling when you walk by, then letting me hear you giggle to your girlfriends the minute you pass out of my peripheral vision. You can bully me rolling your eyes when I answer a question correctly in class. Hell, you can bully me when you don't even know I exist. You can't hurt me physically; you'd have to break the law to hurt me more than I've been hurt. First time I was in foster care, before I even remember, it was because Hector punched me in the stomach. It's in my CPS file. I was three, and he threw me onto the floor to prove to Carline he didn't love me more than her (no proof should have been necessary). He told her he slugged me so hard he thought he felt the floor against his knuckles. *Through me*. I guess *that* proved he loved her. She told on him. It's right there in the file.

Naw, the hurt for me is humiliation. *Threaten* to humiliate me, you *own* me. Problem is, and this doesn't speak highly of my character, if *I* get the chance to bully, I jump on it. Wanna find the biggest pool of bullies? Go where the victims are. Know why? Because bullying feels good. And it feels twice as good if you're the target most of the time. Hence the political incorrectness. I call Rosy fat, Smoky Yardley (and my parents and Herbie Waldron and legions of deserving others) dumb, and Coach Shuster ugly because I don't care. I can say anything I want. *I. Don't. Matter.* If Devin Mack bullies you, you won't even know you're being bullied.

So the threat I face at the far end of this meat-grinder drill isn't the crushing blow about to register inside my helmet. It's the humiliation, the complete sense of incompetence.

Coach slaps the ball into Rich's gut. I get into my three-point stance and wait for the whistle. Rich and I stare past the face masks into each other's eyes.

"Time," Rich yells. He holds up his hand.

"What . . . ?" The whistle drops from Coach's mouth.

You have to be a player of Rich Saxon's status to interrupt one of Coach Bull Shuster's football practices.

Rich drops the ball and walks toward me, motions me to stand. He drapes an arm over my shoulder pads and walks me away from the team. "You can do this," he says.

I can barely breathe. Adrenaline is overflowing, almost buckling my knees. I was *ready*.

He puts his mouth close to my earhole. "Remember what I told you the other night. If you hit me high I bowl you over. If you hit me low you'll get my knee in your helmet." He taps his stomach. "Right below the numbers," he says. "Have faith."

Faith.

"Couldn't you just, like, *go down*?"

"No can do, buddy."

"Why not?"

"This is football," Rich says. "It's what I do. It's who I am. Rich Saxon does not *go down*."

We're headed back toward the drill. Rich slaps my butt. "Faith."

So here's the deal with Rich Saxon. He's about to hurt me. When I hit him I will feel an electric current from my neck down through my feet. My arms, which I'm supposed to wrap around him and hold on for dear life, will be rendered useless at the moment of impact. I will feel my fingertips slide powerlessly down his torso, waist, thigh pads, calves, cleats, air. I will hear the whistle. I will hear, "Again!" But I can't hate him. How do you hate a guy like Rich Saxon? He tried to help me. He told me how to tackle him, gave me my best chance to succeed. But he is thirty-five pounds heavier and at least one evolutionary life-form more adept at this game I have grown to hate.

I don't care about the electricity, don't care about the rush of paralysis, don't care about my body hitting the grass empty-handed. I care about "Again!" and the derisive scowls of my teammates as they watch me drop once more, once more, once more into my three-point stance, many of them grateful it's me and not them, but unwilling to salute my sacrifice.

I hear Rich's voice in my head. "Faith." I take a deep breath. I have faith—faith it will finally get dark, gratitude that our field doesn't have lights.

"Hitter Mack," Rich Saxon says to me a couple of nights ago at Hugo's Little Store.

I recognize irony. "Scaredy-cat Saxon," I say back. It's after eleven p.m., and I've got an hour left in my shift at Hugo's unless the bus is late, in which case I have until it gets here. Greyline Stage comes through every other night, usually before midnight, and Hugo likes to stay open in case some gluttonous passenger wants to load up on Snickers bars and corn chips and ice-cream sandwiches for the last three hours of the trip to Boise. Hugo says if you cater to flatlanders in the off-hours when they really need you, they'll favor your establishment over others when they come back through on their summer weekenders into the sticks. I don't bother to tell Hugo that if you're riding the midnight Greyliner toward Boise in the fall, there's a pretty good chance you don't have the means for a summer week-ender in the sticks, because he's paying me a little under minimum wage and I'm saving every penny I can for my escape fifteen minutes after my high school graduation, which, if Mandy Roberts will let me look over her shoulder on the Latin test, should happen in about two and a half years.

"How you holdin' up?" Rich says now.

"Okay, I guess. How about you?"

"Holdin' up just fine," Rich says.

I nod. "What can I do for you?"

"I'm talkin' about football," he says.

That doesn't quite connect to my question. I can't do anything for Rich Saxon in football.

"When I asked how you're holdin' up. I was talking about football."

"Oh," I say. "Got it. More like needing someone to hold me up, but I'll live."

"You know," he says, "it's all in your head."

I nod.

"And here," he says, thumping his fist against his chest.

I watch him over the counter. "Make a muscle," I say.

"Scuse me?"

"Make a muscle." I point to his right arm. "Pump up your biceps."

He does, and a hardball appears above the crook of his elbow.

I roll up my sleeve and do the same. No hardball. "That's not in my head, Rich. Yours either. It's in your arm. Same with your other arm, same with your legs. . . ."

"Size is not everything," he says. "There's—"

"Speed," I say, "and coordination and quickness—which is not the same as speed—and desire and a certain Cro-Magnon outlook. Rich, I went into a tattoo parlor the other day, asked them for one of those barbed-wire jobs around my right arm? Guy said he'd throw in the other arm free."

"That's funny," Rich says.

"And one calf."

"That's even funnier."

"My talents are wasted on the gridiron."

"I'm serious, man," he says. "You don't look like you're having any fun out there. Football is supposed to be *fun*."

"Lemme buy you a pop," I tell him, feeling kinda special

because Rich Saxon is talking to me like I'm one of the guys. "Take a seat over here in our 'restaurant' section." The restaurant section of Hugo's is a round metal table with four plastic chairs where most people only stop long enough to put mustard on their almost-meat hot dog.

"Gatorade," he says, "but I'll pay for it."

"On me," I say back. "That's why Hugo pays me under minimum. He knows I rip him off to buy friends." I toss Rich a Gatorade.

He twists the cap, guzzles half. "You believe in God?" he asks.

I busy myself stocking shelves close by the table. "I don't know," I say. "What's the difference?"

"Jesus?"

"If you believe in God, I guess you believe in Jesus," I say.

"Only if you're a Christian," he says. "I guess I'm just asking if you have faith."

I don't know why I feel the need to be honest, but I do. I mean, Rich Saxon is hanging out with me. That doesn't happen.

I stop stocking the shelves and look him square in the eye. "Do you?"

"Keeps me going," he says. "I dedicate everything I do to my savior."

Man, could I use a savior. "No offense, Rich, but what does that *mean*?"

"It just means," he says, "He's given me His best and I want to give my best back."

"So you don't, like, ask Him to help us win or something, right? Or point to the sky when you score a TD?"

He gives me a *Duh!* look. "Why would I point to the sky? He knows where He is. No, man, I don't ask Him for anything, especially when it comes to football. What kind of a god would care about a football game when people are starving?"

"An *American* God?"

"You really are funny," Rich says. "Naw, I feel blessed, that's all. So I give it back."

Makes sense, I guess.

"No faith?" Rich asks again.

I start to say I have faith that telling God what I want just gives Him a list of things to make sure I don't get, but I don't want to sound like more of a wuss than I am. "Guess not," I say.

"Not surprised," he says. "I've been watching you on the field, hanging back, trying to stay under Coach's radar. No confidence."

"It's that obvious, huh?"

"Only if you're looking," he says. "You sure aren't the only guy out there trying to keep from getting hurt."

I hold out my arms, look down at my scrawny body. "I'm not afraid to get hurt, Rich. I mean, I don't like it, but I've been . . . well, trust me. I'm not afraid to get hurt."

He sits forward. "What *are* you afraid of?"

I wonder why I feel like crying. "Laughter," I say. "Of the blast of Coach's whistle right before he yells 'Again, Mack!' Then the laughter."

As if on cue the bell above the rickety door jangles and in walks Hector Mack. My old man.

There's a fresh scratch down the side of his face and the faint smell of liquor on his breath—a deadly combination. His glare is trained at me as he takes the first few steps into the store, but he spots Rich and flips his *charm* switch, if you can call it that. "Rich Saxon!" he says. "How you doin', buddy?"

Rich stands, puts out his hand. "I'm okay, Mr. Mack. How are you?"

Dad shoots a sideways glance at me, but . . . "Good. I'm good. You guys gonna be league champs this year?"

Rich smiles. "It'd be the first time this century," he says. "But it's possible, I guess."

Dad gestures his head toward me. "Guess you won't

be gettin' much help from Mr. Football here," he says. "Worthless as a toothless pit bull." He laughs, showing an equal number of existing and missing teeth. That passes for humor in Hector's world.

Rich flinches. "Actually, I think he'll do us a lot of good. He's comin' right along."

"Shee . . . comin' along to the end of the bench. He hasn't even been in a game."

"Not yet, maybe," Rich says. "But he'll see some action before the year's over. An' he's got two more years. Lotta guys don't play at first."

"You was startin' your freshman year."

"Yeah, well, I was big for my age. And my parents held me back a year."

Dad won't be denied. He's hacked off big time about something and not even the presence of a high school football hero is going to keep it down forever. In his *soul* he's gotta disgrace me.

"You work hard at football," he says. He's talking to Rich, but looking at me.

"Yes, sir, I do."

"I can't even get my little girl to do the dishes." He raises his eyebrows at me.

"I told you, Hector, we practiced late. I had to get to

136

work. I didn't even dirty any."

"Yeah, well, that got the ol' lady on my butt."

I look at the scratch, probably smile. "I see that."

Suddenly he has me by the front of the shirt. "You think that's funny?" He draws back his hand. I unfocus and wait for the *bang*, only wishing Rich Saxon wouldn't see this. I can take the hit. . . .

Rich catches Dad's arm in midswing, and Dad whirls, ready to go. But he must have the same thought I'll have tomorrow standing at one end of the meat grinder, facing Rich on the other. Rich Saxon dwarfs my father.

"Get your hand off me! You can't touch me!"

"You can't touch *him*." Rich's voice is steady, calm.

"He's my kid. I'll touch 'im anytime I want to!"

Rich shakes his head. "You won't touch him now."

"Big football hero," Dad says, releasing my shirt. "We'll see about this. I got rights. I'm his damn *parent*." He turns and storms out.

We stand, watching the door swing shut.

There's no way to dress this up. I want to say I'm sorry he had to see that, but the words dry on my tongue before I can spit them out. Rich puts a hand on my shoulder. "Wow," he says.

"Yeah."

"Listen, man, you wanna spend the night at my place? We have an extra room."

"Naw, he'll be asleep by the time I get home. Or in a coma if he goes back and messes with my mom. I won't get the backlash from this until next time. Dumb as my old man is, he never forgets a slight."

Rich pulls his letter jacket off the back of the plastic chair. "Sure? I can drop you by your house to get some stuff."

"I'm sure. Got it covered."

That's how I lose friends. I mean, all things considered, I could get along okay. People think I'm funny sometimes. I make sure I never invite anyone home, and figure out a way to always wear clean clothes. But there are 867 people in this town and sooner or later anybody who considers being my friend sees either Mom or Dad go after me. It's a crazy thing about humans—being treated bad makes them hate *you*.

I drop into my three-point stance once more as Rich walks back toward Coach, take a deep breath, and get ready for a long afternoon. Coach smacks Rich with the ball again, and sucks air, ready to blast that whistle. Rich looks past my face mask one more time, and I guess he's not satisfied, 'cause he puts his hand up once more. "Time."

Coach has about had it. Even for Rich Saxon.

Rich hands him the ball again, walks toward me, motions me up.

"Man," I say, "just lemme get this over with."

"I'm lookin' in your eyes, Mack; I don't see it, man. You got faith?"

I shake my head. "Got no faith, Rich."

"Gotta have faith. Not in God. In yourself. When you hear that whistle, you come at me with everything you *got,* hear me?"

"I hear you, Rich."

"I mean it." He grabs my face mask. "Look at me."

What am I gonna do? He's got my face mask. I look at him.

"*Everything* you've got. Right below my numbers. Shoulder first, and wrap me up like you're holding on to a life buoy in a hurricane."

"Shoulder first. Life buoy," I say.

"Faith," he says.

"Shoulder," I say again. "Life buoy."

The whistle blasts and Rich explodes at me, knees high, legs pumping like pistons. And I give him everything I've got. I'm running low, staring right at his waistline. In the distance I hear a guttural growl, realize just before impact it's coming out of *me*.

A light explodes in my head; all feeling drains from my extremities. My arms try to wrap him up, but they are disconnected from my brain. I open my eyes in time to see his legs churning on past, close them again, and wait for sensation to return. And the whistle.

Precious few acts of kindness have been directed my way in my lifetime, so few I bet I remember them all. I don't say that to get sympathy or pity; it's just fact. But none like this. In the same second Rich runs me over, he stops on a dime, whirls, and hurdles my near-lifeless body back to Coach in time to snatch the whistle from between his lips. "Pound for pound," he says, "that's the hardest I've ever been hit." He nods toward me. "How 'bout it, Coach? My buddy Mack's done with this drill for the day."

Coach stares at me. His whistle blasts. "Next up!"

THE CHOICE
BY JAMES BROWN

I was in seventh grade when I first saw Bill Bradley playing basketball on our television in the basement. I didn't know it then, but watching him would influence the path of my life.

In some ways, I was lucky to see him at all. We didn't watch much television in our modest home in Washington, DC. My father worked two jobs and stayed busy supporting us, and my mother the homemaker made sure that we understood that we needed to work hard to be successful in life.

We needed to work hard on our school studies, needed to work hard around the house, and we simply needed to work hard and excellently at whatever we did. I certainly carried that work ethic over to sports, which I loved.

I was not an overnight success in sports. I had a lot of potential but had to work diligently in sharpening the fundamentals to become a good player, not ever thinking about stardom. Before high school, I made my basketball team in eighth grade, not because I was a great player, but because I was a good listener and the coach loved the fact that I paid attention and he knew I was going to be a hard worker. I was a role player even then. I did my part to make the rest of the team better.

Unfortunately for me, my role in those days was to set a good example of being a good listener and being coachable—but nothing that I did on the court. In fact, on the day when we were introduced to the student body, we dribbled down the court to make a layup . . . and I blew the uncontested layup. I still remember the gymnasium full of my peers, laughing. I was looking for a place to hide. Not the way you play it out in your fantasies. At least, not the way that I did.

In fact, before I ever became serious about my basketball, my first love was baseball. I've got a picture of me playing Catholic Youth Organization (CYO) baseball when I was fifteen years old. The picture captures me perfectly at that time: long and lanky, my uniform hanging off me, the unique nose that is undeniably mine.

I looked like a human coat hanger, skinny and pointy.

I hit a lot of home runs in the CYO play-offs that summer, and Morgan Wootten, a famous basketball coach from DeMatha Catholic High School in Hyattsville, Maryland, was in attendance. He was there to see a pitcher on our team, a blond-haired guy named Steve Garrett who threw really hard and was headed to DeMatha for ninth grade the next year. Steve was a great three-sport athlete in football, baseball, and basketball and, to cap it all off, was also a good student. Coach was there to watch three games in the play-offs. And as I recall, Steve threw a perfect game, a one-hitter, and a no-hitter. No wonder Coach Wootten felt pretty good about the decision to have Steve attend DeMatha. After the weekend, when Steve's leverage with DeMatha couldn't have been any higher, Steve brought Coach Wootten over to meet me. "Coach, this is our left fielder, James Brown." Coach greeted me and asked if I played basketball also since I was such a big kid. I did, I told him. "I scored one point last season for my eighth-grade team."

Coach Wootten nodded. "I'll talk with the baseball coach for you," he said. He obviously didn't have any need for me on the basketball court.

Coach Wootten did talk to the baseball coach, and I was accepted. My parents were ecstatic, as DeMatha is a private school that would require a financial sacrifice but provide the academic foundation my parents preached was important. Although it was in Maryland, it was located only a few miles outside of DC. Before I arrived at DeMatha, though, I attended a summer basketball camp with Coach Wootten because I knew I needed help with my skills to progress on the basketball court—I still wanted to play basketball. I took everything he said to heart about sharpening my skills, so much that I quit playing baseball and focused exclusively on basketball from that time forward.

I think my dad might have been a little disappointed, but he never did anything but encourage me. Family legend maintains that my father stood over my crib with my uncle admiring my right arm and dreaming of the day when I would be an ace pitcher. I hated to disappoint him, but I realized that, even during that summer of hitting home run upon home run in CYO baseball, I had no future in the game. Steve Garrett and his heat-seeking missile of a fastball helped me to quickly come to that realization. And to make matters worse, he had a big, sharp-breaking curveball! I vividly remember standing in the batter's box during an intrasquad game, watching him throw to me the pitches

I've seen him throw to opposing batters so many times. He threw me a breaking ball—I read the spin of the pitch coming out of his hand and knew it was a curveball. As usual, he started the pitch inside, coming at the hitter—in this case, me. I was talking myself through it after seeing that spin. *It's gonna break. Wait for it. It's about to break. It's gonna break. Isn't it going to break? Is it going to break? IT'S NOT GOING TO BREAK!* my brain screamed as I hit the dirt, skinny arms and legs flying in every direction.

Sure enough, it broke over the plate for a strike.

That's when I realized I didn't have the courage to stand in the batter's box as I got bigger and guys started throwing harder and harder. Steve and his breaking ball—they conspired to get me out of the game.

So I soaked up every pearl of wisdom during Coach Wootten's summer camp, every drill he taught, every axiom he conveyed. I used to joke that the rich tan you see me sporting now is the result of me working relentlessly on my basketball game outdoors for three or four hours a day in the blazing hot sun. My becoming one of the best leapers in the District of Columbia was in some part genetics, but mostly because I went berserk on the exercises (toe raises) that I had been told would improve my jumping ability—and they did.

* * *

Four years after seeing Bill Bradley for the first time, my own recruitment in college basketball came in 1969. It was three years after the college basketball game that caused a seismic shift on the collegiate landscape: the 1966 National Championship game in which underdog Texas Western and their all-black starting five beat the powerhouse University of Kentucky and their all-white starting five. It seems hard to imagine now that a game like that really happened, but it did. By the time I came along, all schools were recruiting players regardless of their color—even Kentucky offered me a scholarship.

All of us in the Brown family knew we were going to college, which strikes me as impressive, looking back. It seemed so normal at the time that our parents, who did not attend college themselves, would have very firm expectations that we would do so. In fact, a big part of the reason that my dad worked so hard at his different jobs each day was so that my mom could stay home to be the superb homemaker that she was and to instill in us an attitude of excellence. Mom was smart and disciplined and wanted each of her kids to go further in life than she and Dad did. She was going to make sure that her children were educated to their fullest.

As colleges started showing interest in me, Coach Wootten took me aside. He had seen so many great players come through his gym and go on to play college basketball that he wanted to make certain that I knew what to expect. As the first to go to college in my family, and as a boy who wanted to please everyone by nature, his advice was greatly appreciated.

"When you visit a school," he told me, "they're going to show you the best of everything. They set you up, by design, in the perfect honeymoon situation. Therefore, you just *cannot* commit when you are on campus. Leave the school and come home to discuss the decision with your family. If you still feel the same way after twenty-four hours, then commit."

Coach wasn't kidding. I was treated so well on every single visit. Nice accommodations, lobster dishes, which I loved, and other fancy meals, none of which were an issue back when I was eighteen and six feet five inches tall and a skinny 210 pounds. I have to be a little more careful with the drawn butter these days!

I called Coach from Chapel Hill, home of the University of North Carolina. I had a great visit with Dean Smith, and loved the school and the program. I also admired Coach Smith and his inclusive approach to coaching and recruiting . . . aggressively going after the best student-athletes—black *and* white. I told Coach Wootten that I wasn't going to commit on campus, but UNC was where I wanted to attend school. We agreed that I should tell Coach Smith that I was 99 percent sure that I would attend but needed to go home and speak with my family.

A few days later, I saw a letter from Harvard sitting on Coach Wootten's desk—for me. Immediately, I thought of what Bill Bradley had done at Princeton. I thought that *if* I could get *into* Harvard, perhaps I could do the same. Bill Bradley, the Princeton great, was then playing for the Knicks. I probably would have preferred the letter be from Princeton because of my respect for Bradley, and would have probably signed on the spot. As it was, Harvard was immediately elevated in my mind to that position next to Carolina. My mom didn't try to push me one way or the other. She just wanted me to fully capitalize on the educational opportunity in front of me.

In the process, I took trips to St. Bonaventure, Notre Dame, Michigan, Harvard, and North Carolina. I didn't take an official trip to Maryland because it was local and easy to visit; but their coach, Lefty Driesell, made his interest clear when he took out a billboard in DC picturing the top four high school players, including me. Flattering, but

I was focused on Harvard and North Carolina.

Now, many people thought that Harvard pulled out all the stops when it pulled out a weapon that Carolina couldn't match: Ted Kennedy. Senator Kennedy, a US Senator from Massachusetts and the youngest brother of our assassinated president John F. Kennedy, contacted Coach Wootten and arranged for a car to come get us and take us to Capitol Hill to meet him. We visited with him in his office, watched him cast a couple of votes in the Senate, and before the day was out, I promised that I would visit Harvard before deciding. As impressive as Senator Kennedy was, the more influential Harvard alumni were former Secretary of the Army Clifford Alexander and successful DC businessman Barry Linde. Getting to know them on a personal level really sealed the deal for me, as both had come from more modest backgrounds like I had.

Red Auerbach, the legendary Boston Celtics coach and executive, was a great friend of DeMatha High and Coach Wootten. Even he weighed in on my college choice. Well, kind of. He grinned at me and told me, "James, remember this: there is only one Harvard." He didn't exactly tell me where to go, but he did leave it at that. I got the message. From my mom to basketball executives—everything looked Crimson. Even my siblings were starting to come around. Well, kind of. My brothers thought it would be so cool to have a brother who was a Tar Heel and therefore were still pulling for UNC and Dean Smith to win the recruiting battle. They do remember Ted Kennedy coming by the house, though, and the impression it made on them, even four decades later.

It was still a tough decision because of how much I liked Chapel Hill and Coach Smith; and the University of North Carolina is an excellent school as well.

In the meantime, Coach Wootten called me into his office. "James, how many colleges do you plan on going to next year?" I looked at him, confusion on my face. He went on. "This morning was the fifth call I've gotten from a coach—North Carolina, Maryland, Michigan, and others—who told me that you're '99 percent sure' that you're coming to his school."

I grimaced.

"James, you're going to learn, at some point in your life, to tell somebody no."

I don't think that I have yet.

I was still wrestling with the decision. I lost track because of the magnitude of the overall numbers, but my brothers and sister have said that I was being recruited by upward of two hundred schools. Letters were coming in every day from all parts of the country, and I was still unable to decide.

Harvard loomed large in my mind because of the emphasis that my mom and dad placed on academic excellence being the number one priority for us. Coach Auerbach was right—there is only one Harvard. Mom would ask me, "What if you break your leg and can't play basketball again? Wherever you go to school, if you excel in the classroom, you'll always have that to fall back on." She stressed, "What you put between your ears will determine how successful you will be."

I was also still intrigued by the chance to follow in the footsteps of Bill Bradley, the man whom I admired so greatly. He had graduated from Princeton in 1965, a three-time All-American who had led the school to a number three final national ranking following the NCAA Tournament. He was named the top amateur athlete in the United States in 1965. And it was readily apparent, from Bradley's college career and subsequent NBA career with the New York Knicks, that a player could be no less successful on the court coming out of an Ivy League school.

I had watched him arrive at the Knicks in 1966, my ninth-grade year and the year of the historic game between Texas Western and Kentucky. I had read about his work ethic: he took thousands of shots from all over the court, working on his game every day. He never wanted to receive special treatment and passed up the chance to earn lots of money making commercials and being a company spokesman. He just wanted to spend his time becoming the best basketball player that he could.

I, too, wanted to be an inspiration. In addition to every other reason my family had for me to attend Harvard, I wanted to be a role model. As a young man born into modest circumstances, I wanted to be a role model for kids in similar circumstances and show that the sky was the limit for them. I wanted to be a part of something very special at Harvard . . . to show that academic excellence could go hand in hand with athletic success. That success like that would make them champions in the game of Life. I wanted to show that there were black athletes who were concerned with things beyond athletic success.

By no means am I a charter member of Mensa, and I didn't perform particularly well on standardized tests. What I did, however, was work assiduously at my studies. Where it might take another student thirty minutes to grasp the material, I might need four hours. I didn't let it beat me, however; I was willing to spend as much time as it took, and knew that I would eventually master whatever material was assigned. I knew that I could work hard enough to do well academically at any school.

After agonizing over the decision, I finally settled on Harvard. The school was kind enough to ease the intense recruiting pressure by giving me an early-admission answer. I accepted and said that I would attend.

That's when the letter arrived that had me jumping through the roof and appealing to my family to allow me *one more* college visit because I'd received an envelope with "UCLA" written in deep sky blue and sun gold.

"Mom, this is from UCLA. I have to go. I have to at least visit. Pauley Pavilion. John Wooden. It's U . . . C . . . L . . . A." I said it slowly, enunciating each letter, as if she was having trouble with my spelling. "It's the Mecca of college basketball. They dominate college basketball—they've won two straight National Championships and four of the last five!"

Coach Wootten was always quoting John Wooden, UCLA's Hall of Fame coach. "It takes ten hands to make one basket," he'd quote Coach Wooden, reminding us that all five players were important.

However, my mother was unmoved. My father, too. They sat me down. "James, you have given your word to Harvard. Your word means more than anything, son. You shook hands and said that you were coming. You cannot change your mind now. You're going to Harvard."

And so I told UCLA that I was headed to Harvard, and went up to Cambridge to play for Bob Harrison. Coach Harrison was an NBA All-Star and had played for the old Minneapolis Lakers, Milwaukee Hawks, St. Louis Hawks, and Syracuse Nationals. He came a year earlier from Kenyon College, a program that he had turned around, and arrived with great expectations of doing at Harvard what had happened at Princeton and Pennsylvania. My sophomore year, when we finished 11–3 in the Ivy League and had K. C. Jones, the Celtics great, as an assistant coach, we had our best season—still not as successful, though, as we had hoped. Our team was a talent-laden one, with enough potential to have contended for the Ivy League title each year. Indeed, we were expected to put Harvard basketball on the path to national prominence like those other Ivy League schools had enjoyed. We were ranked the second-best incoming freshman class in the nation in 1969 (freshmen couldn't play varsity in those days) and had our highest preseason ranking ever the next year, when we were finally eligible to play. Instead, we were mediocre and contributed to the dismissal of Coach Harrison in 1973, as we were graduating.

One game from my college career stands out. We were playing across the Charles River, at Boston University. BU had a couple of players also from Washington, DC, so it had a hometown rivalry feel for me even though it was in Boston. That was probably my best individual game, as I was in a zone all night, scoring thirty-six points in a 104–77 win for the Crimson. At that time, I was not a great, consistent outside scorer, but I was shooting and scoring from all over the court. It was one of those nights when I could take three or four steps across midcourt and shoot . . . and score. I say "one of those nights," but come to think of it, that was probably the only night of my life like that! Long jumpers from all over, nothing but the bottom of the net. And those thirty-six points came at a time when college basketball didn't have a three-point line, either.

Of course, with my outfit that day, I had no choice but to play well. We went over to BU's gymnasium and walked around campus for a while. The movie *Super Fly* had just been released that year, and I showed up on BU's campus wearing a full-length white leather coat. However, to make the coat truly classy, it had gray faux fur around the hem and the collar. It looked like something Clyde Frazier would wear, only he would have had real fur on! And a hat to match. Did I mention that I also wore red zip-up boots and gray bell-bottom pants? If you're going to do it, go from head to toe! It really made a statement. I shudder to think just what that statement was that I was making to the Harvard alumni who traveled across the river to see the game.

It was certainly a different take on the fur coats usually being worn at Harvard games.

My overall Harvard experience was outstanding, and our lack of success on the court was my only regret—it still pains me to think of our struggles after the promise with which we entered. We entered with a couple of high school All-Americans and several All-State players, but we never put it together. I wish I had applied the same work ethic that I did in high school and after college.

Between the times of political unrest on campus and our disappointing play on the basketball court, we simply never fulfilled our potential. However, when it's all said and done, the ultimate responsibility lay with me. I knew from high school what it took to be successful. Players are made in the off-season. But when guys from other schools were working all summer getting better, I wasn't. I had plenty of excuses available—the academic course load made it impossible to enjoy sustained basketball excellence at Harvard—but it doesn't matter. It's up to the individual.

Some of the other good memories from those times consisted of seeing my family who went to school in the Boston area. My brother John attended Curry College in Milton, Massachusetts, just south of Boston. The way my sister tells it, Mom told Alicia that she could go to any school she wanted to . . . in Massachusetts. She ended up attending Emerson College in Boston, which meant that by my senior year, three of us were in school in Massachusetts. For my youngest brother, Everett, however, this meant a significant number of eight-hour drives with Mom and Dad from DC to Boston to visit us and see games. Although he enjoyed being in the locker room and going to the games, Everett said that he was sick of Boston by the time we got out of school. I always enjoyed having them nearby.

It made being so far from home much more tolerable. As it was, those four years marked the only time I would ever live outside of the DC area—my home.

Although our team wasn't as good as we would have hoped, I performed well enough to be named to the All-Ivy League team for three consecutive seasons and was drafted by the Atlanta Hawks of the NBA and the Denver Rockets of the ABA. I chose to sign with the Hawks but was cut by the team before the first regular-season game.

I couldn't believe it. I was sure that I was going to be

like Bill Bradley and play many years in the NBA, and be a role model for other kids. I was crushed and cried for days. Weeks, maybe. I went back to my parents' home and wouldn't come out of my room.

Finally, I quit feeling sorry for myself and got to work. I went into business and then started working a second job: broadcasting NBA games in Washington for $250 a game. Those games led to opportunities on local television and then to a chance to broadcast on national television. After fifteen years of working my way up, I was blessed to cohost the FOX NFL Sunday pregame show and today am thrilled to host the *NFL Today* pregame show on CBS and *Inside the NFL* on Showtime, and others.

My basketball talent got me into Harvard, and my hard work in learning as much as I could at Harvard prepared me for all of the fun opportunities God has opened up for me since.

My parents were right: focusing on getting the best possible education truly has provided me with the foundation to have enjoyed much more in life than I could have ever dreamed.

Thanks, Mom and Dad.

CHOKE
BY JOSEPH BRUCHAC

How did I get here? That's a question most of us have asked ourselves at one time or another. But not about the situation in which I now find myself: standing across the ring from someone who looks twice my width despite us both having weighed in at 165 pounds on the button. Not only that, but as the referee has us touch our gloves at the center of the ring, Tipper Sodaman leans forward with a grin as friendly as a mako shark's.

"This time, fish, I'm going to gut you."

How nice of him to remind me—just in case I could have somehow forgotten having my face pushed down into a pile of dog poop behind the football bleachers—that we had met before. How fun to renew old friendships a year later!

I don't answer him, of course. That would be bad form according to all of my teachers, men who've been in this sort of situation themselves.

Oh really? my inner voice replies.

Shut up, inner voice.

But I do whisper to myself as I go back to my corner, "It doesn't matter if I win or lose. Just as long as I don't choke."

Oh really?

Inner voice, if you don't cool it, I am going to kick your butt.

I'm not here to prove myself.

Then what are you here for? asks that sardonic inner voice.

There's just enough time for me to think back an answer that I believe to be the right one.

Because.

And then to ask myself one more time that same damn question.

How the heck did I get here?

It is not a long story. It's so short that I can relate it to you as the two of us approach each other to meet in the center of the ring.

Let me begin by making it perfectly clear that I was not a scrawny 98-pound weakling when, at the age of fifteen,

I decided to devote myself to mixed martial arts. I tipped the rusty bathroom scale—which was at least as reliable as a congenital liar—at a full 104 pounds. That weight, I concluded, combined with my bony height of six feet three inches, meant that I was well equipped to become a deadly ninja-type warrior. For it is widely known that ninjas can make themselves invisible. All I had to do was turn sideways to more or less vanish. And I was hardly in need of weapons, for as my little sister, Maggie, so supportively observed, I was so bony that I could disembowel someone by just bumping into them with my hips.

If a sense of humor—or self-deprecating sarcasm—was a weapon, then my entire family would be deadly warriors.

"It is just your Slovak blood," my mother helpfully observed as she passed by our diminutive bathroom, which, lacking an actual door, might be better described as a family showroom. True, everyone else politely averts their eyes when someone is in there. But my mother, being the mother, assumes that she is exempt from such considerations as recognizing her children's desire for privacy. That is why Maggie, a popular and perky fourteen-year-old, never applied makeup at home but lugged her whole kit—which weighed as much as I do—with her to school in her backpack.

"We Slovaks," Mom continued, "we are slow to thicken. We start thin. Like Johnn Little Pea. Like the oak tree, we take time to put down roots. Weeds grow fast and stay small. Trees take time and get big."

I know Mom was trying to build me up. She knew, as did everyone in the universe, about my recent dismal athletic failure.

The football team I'd tried to join that fall had been so full of weeds—older boys and kids my age with twice my bulk—that I was choked out from the first moment I set foot on the field. Maybe I would have found a way to fit in if I'd been allowed to stick with it longer than the two weeks I suffered being dissed by everyone, beginning with the equipment manager. When I held a tackling dummy, I was not only knocked over by the first guy who hit it but sent rolling for a good twenty feet with my spidery arms and legs wrapped around the dummy. The line coach looked at me with a combination of pity and contempt that made me feel lower than a gopher's basement. And when I not only failed to catch the ball that was tossed to me by the second-string quarterback, but also allowed it to hit me square in the forehead, leaving a red mark that morphed into a big purple bruise, the offensive coach wrote me off like a bad debt.

The head coach took me aside after that.

"Son," he said, "I admire your spirit. I've never seen a kid less athletic who's tried harder. But you are going to have to quit now. Otherwise you are going to end up getting really hurt."

"Why?" I asked. "You mean my blood isn't good enough to keep fertilizing your football field?"

The coach almost laughed, but he shook his head instead. "There it is," he said. "Your mouth. The way you keep making remarks like that. That's what really makes this too dangerous for you. If I don't kick you off this team, someday one of those other kids who's not as smart as you is going to kill you because of something you said."

It was when I was coming out of the back of the building on the other side of the field after turning in my ill-fitting uniform that I ran into Tipper Sodaman, stocky, simian-shaped starting right linebacker.

Several of his buddies were behind him. All of them equally anthropoid.

"What's the matter, fish?" Tipper said. "Quitting 'cause you're scared?"

I spread my arms to show I had no intention of responding in an angry fashion. "No," I said with a friendly smile, "I just seem to have too much crane in me and not enough gorilla."

He took my remark as sarcasm. Which, to be fair, it was.

Sadly, perhaps because *Rise of the Planet of the Apes* had just hit the theaters, he knew what a gorilla was.

"You calling me an ape?" he said, stepping forward and throwing me down before I had the opportunity to reply. The fact that my mouth was open to make said reply meant that I more or less ate a good bit of the pile of dog doo-doo in which my face was thrust.

As I sat up, spitting it out, he and his gang walked away from me in disgust. I doubt that they heard me say "But I prefer Alpo." Nor did they see me sit there for at least five minutes more, my chest heaving as I cried my heart out.

When you have been undone by your lack of physical prowess and your overabundance of quick repartee, it helps to have understanding parents. If they weren't incredibly understanding, they would not have signed the waiver that has allowed me, underage as I am, to step into this ring to take part in an amateur mixed martial arts contest.

"Dad," I said, "I need to learn how to fight."

My father took one look at me—and probably one smell, for I had failed to get all of the poodle poop out of my hair—and understood.

"Want boxing lessons?" My father had boxed in the navy and, though he never bragged about it, had been good. I'd found the medals he'd won one day by accident when he

asked me to bring him a shirt from his closet and I accidentally tipped over the cigar box he had them stashed in.
Gold and silver every one of them.

"More than that," I said. "I want to be like Anderson
Silva."

"The Spider?"

"You got it, Dad!" I'm pleased he knew my reference
to the Brazilian MMA fighter. He's the best in the world,
pound for pound.

"Want to take a ride?"

I'm always a little surprised at the number of people my
dad knows. Maybe it's because his job as a news editor at
our paper takes him around to so many places. And maybe
that job is why his conversational style is invariably inter-
rogatory. The next thing I knew, we were pulling up in
front of the storefront of what once was a neighborhood
corner grocery but now had the words EAST COUNTRY MMA
on the window in small letters.

"You want to go inside?"

"Only as much as I want to keep breathing."

The wide floor was covered with blue mats. The walls
that had once held display cases were covered with mirrors.
And there was a boxing ring in the far right corner, an

MMA cage in the far left.

The rangy man who came loping up to shake my dad's hand had a craggy face that looked like it had been through more than one storm but still emerged like a peak from the clouds to reflect the sun.

"Jao, how are you?" my father said, holding out his hand as Jao took it with both of his.

"Good, Frank. This your boy?"

Dad nudged me, and I stepped forward.

"Johnny," I said, holding out my own hand.

Jao took it, again with both hands. His grasp wasn't one of those crush-your-fist grips that so many men use to prove their strength. But it was firm enough to make me feel that if he held on, there was no way I could pull away. *He's a jaguar,* I thought. Don't ask me why. Then, with the lazy certainty of one of those big predatory cats, he locked his eyes on mine. I felt as if he were reading my mind. Something like an electric pulse ran down my back. He let go and then clapped both hands on my shoulders, punched my chest with the flat of his right palm, and then stepped back.

"Hmm," he said, looking me up and down.

And even though this was the point where the usual me would have made a sarcastic remark—like maybe "Be careful you don't cut yourself on my ribs"—my mouth stayed shut.

"Think you can do something with him, Maestre?" Dad said.

"Sure. If he wants."

"You want?" Dad asked.

"Yes, sir," I said.

"You know you're going to have to pay for it out of your own savings?"

"I know," I said, thinking there was no better way than this to spend the bucks I'd earned packing groceries at the Saveco.

"Tomorrow," Jao said. "Beginner's class. Six p.m. You bring mouthpiece, shorts, cup. Okay? Now we fit you for gi. Make it nice and roomy so you grow into it. Thirty-five dollars." Jao held out his hand and I took it again, realizing as soon I did so that I was being my typical stupid self because he was clearly asking me for payment rather than another friendly handshake.

But instead of making fun of me, Jao pulled me closer so that our chests bumped and laughed in a way that made me laugh along with him.

"I think you got a good boy here," Maestre Jao said.

"You think?" my dad said, reaching into his pocket and

pulling out the thirty-five dollars that he counted into my new teacher's hand.

"'Pay me back when we get home?" Dad asked as we walked toward the back of the room, where a small shop was set up offering various martial arts gear including a rack of white gis.

"Yes, sir," I said. This was the longest I had gone since I had learned to talk without saying more than two words at a time. But also knowing I was saying just enough.

To say that first class I attended was the hardest workout in my life would be like saying that the sea was somewhat moist. We began by running in place for five minutes, then did about fifty thousand stomach crunches (I lost count after twenty), a million push-ups, and twenty or thirty more muscle-building and stretching exercises I had never heard of before. Somehow I stuck it out, even though I felt alternately like a limp dishrag and a rubber band about to snap. The room was full of people—twenty-four others in addition to me—and they ranged from kids my age or younger to people with graying hair. Mostly men, but a few very determined-looking women, too. And no one I knew, thank the gods.

I'd learn later that most kids my age preferred to study

MMA at the Pit Bull Fight Pit way on the other side of town, where the motto was "Bite my leg off. I'll just use it to club you to death."

That workout took us forty minutes. I collapsed on my back feeling pretty good about having survived my first MMA lesson.

"Okay," Maestre Jao said. "Good warm-up. Now we start class."

Before I go further, let me explain very carefully that I was not Daniel-san to Maestre Jao's Mr. Miyagi. I was not taken on for any reason other than that I wanted to be a student and I could pay my monthly fee to his academy. Jao loved what he taught, but he also had to pay the rent and so he ran the academy as a businessman does. No pay, no play. And I was not his special student. I was just one of more than sixty students at various stages, each of us paying our hundred dollars a month. (I would be bagging groceries for a long time to rebuild my savings account.) No sentimental attachments. But that does not mean Jao did not care. To Jao, every student was a special student as long as Jao saw that the student's heart was in it as much as his body. And his staff of instructors had that same philosophy, as well as a respect for every style of fighting. Max, the boxing instructor, was a Golden Gloves champ at light

JOSEPH BRUCHAC

heavyweight. Phil, who taught wrestling takedowns and defenses, was a wrestling coach at the nearby junior college. And then there was Vikorn, who had a typically short but meteoric career in Muay Thai in his native land and had then immigrated to America to work as the manager of his uncle's restaurant. All of them seemed to share that same aura of mutual regard and tough self-assurance that I hoped would someday be mine as well.

Unlike some Brazilian jiujitsu black belts who follow the old Gracie line of "our martial art is the best of all," Jao had trained in many styles, from boxing and Greco-Roman wrestling to kickboxing and Muay Thai. His lineage and black belt were from Carlson Gracie—whose photo was on the wall of Jao's office—but he had been a successful mixed martial artist and knew that jiujitsu was not enough. He explained that one evening as a few of us sat around with him after our evening two-hour training session. By now I was able to speak more than two words at a time in his academy. And it was that night when I earned a nickname from him, one that was not just from my skinny limbs—which were actually putting on some muscle—but also from the way I was able to wrap my partners up, especially in what were now my two favorite moves: the triangle and the rear-naked choke. I was still not strong enough to always tap someone out, but I was

174

good enough to give a good roll.

"So what's the best way to fight?" someone sitting behind me asked. It was a new student whose name I hadn't learned, an eager guy from the nearby naval base who had been to two classes thus far and who—like 50 percent of the people who came to the academy—would quit before putting in a second month.

Jao lifted up his thumb. "Man know only boxing, he get beat by kickboxer, wrestler, Muay Thai, jiujitsu."

He looked around our little circle. We all nodded.

Then he held up his thumb and his index finger. "Know only kickboxing, he get beat by wrestler, maybe, too, by jiujitsu fighter. Maybe beat Muay Thai fighter."

He sat back, letting it sink in. But he was not finished. He held up two index fingers.

"Wrestler knows only wrestling, he goes against jiu-jitsu?" The pause was a question, and I dared to answer it.

"Guillotine choke," I said in a soft voice.

Jao beamed. "Right. But what if a man who knows boxing and wrestling and Muai Thai and kickboxing goes against a man who knows only jiujitsu."

"Oops," I replied before I could stop myself.

It was the closest I'd dared get to my old sarcasm, but in response Jao leaned forward and patted my shoulder. "Yes, Little Spider," he said. The name stuck. But that wasn't all he gave me that evening.

"What if someone is a lot stronger than you?" Navy guy again, of course.

Jao chuckled. "Always assume that anyone you fight is stronger than you. Then you can find his weakness."

I nodded. Jao may not be Mr. Miyagi, but he knew his stuff. He even lasted a round and a half against my idol, Anderson Silva, when he was a pro.

I filed it away in the long list of mental notes I'd made for myself. Like doing my best to not use what we learn in here in school or on the street. Like keeping my mouth shut and taking another route to my classes when I see Tipper and his buddies coming my way and bragging about all the MMA they've been learning at the PBFP.

The year went by faster than I'd expected. And not a single confrontation at school due to my new success at truly making myself invisible. Which is, I guess, why Tipper's jaw dropped when he saw me in the opposite corner and realized who he was about to fight. But it only dropped for a second before it turned into that shark-like grin. Easy meat, he clearly thought.

As we advance toward each other across the ring, I'm crouched low, but not so low that I can't move quickly to get out of the way.

No elbows, I'm thinking.

That was what the ref said in our instructions. Right after the ring announcer reminded everyone that this was an amateur bout, three two-minute rounds.

"Remember, guys, this is amateur, not the UFC. No elbows."

So, of course, that is what my old lunch buddy Tipper tries right away. After feinting a jab, he steps in with a spinning elbow that would have split my face wide-open.

If I'd been there, that is. I step back as he is spinning and watch him lose his balance when his illegal strike fails to connect. He stumbles back into the referee, who grabs his arm and shakes a finger in front of his nose.

"No elbows, son! Got it?"

What Tipper wants to get is me. He pushes off from the ref and charges, to be met by the punch that both Max and my dad have told me is the best weapon in a long-armed fighter's arsenal.

The left jab.

I pump it three times: head, chest, head again. It doesn't do any real damage but makes Tipper step back in confusion. He circles me, a little warier after finding out that this guppy has teeth.

"Good, Spider! Keep your distance," Jao calls to me from my corner. "Feel him out."

Good advice, but Tipper charges me and shoots for a double-leg takedown so fast that all I can do is sprawl. In addition to his recent MMA training, Tipper is also the varsity 165-pound wrestler, so his try is no joke. But I hook under his arm with a whizzer, push on his head with my other hand, and I'm free. To my surprise, strong as I know Tipper to be, he's not that much stronger than me.

He stares at me as I slide back. "I am going to bust you up!" he snarls.

I almost reply, "You and what army." But I don't.

Stay focused, my inner voice says, trying to be helpful. It's not. Sometimes, like in a fight, thinking is the worst thing you can do.

"Spider, act and react," Jao shouts. "You hear me, Spider? Act and react."

Before I can do either one, Tipper hits me square in the belly with a side kick. It doesn't knock the wind out of me. All those stomach crunches—about a billion by now—have made me rock hard there. But the leg sweep that he follows it up with takes my legs out from under me, and I land on my back.

Next thing I know, a screaming wolverine is on top of me, swinging one punch after another. Or maybe it's a chimpanzee. No, it's actually Tipper. But I have my hands up, block one punch after another, then grab his wrist, throw one foot over his back as I push against his thigh with the other foot, and pivot. Voilà! Tipper is swept, and I am on top in full mount.

And before I can do anything else, the bell sounds and the round is over.

I jump up to my feet and reach a hand down to help Tipper up. To my surprise—and his—he grabs my hand, lets me pull him up. Then he realizes what he's done. He drops my paw like a hot potato and spins away from me as fast as he can, backing into his own corner.

Round two. Someone was talking to me in the corner between rounds. It takes me a minute to realize it was my father.

"Great job, son. Now use your range. Keep stuffing his takedowns and then pick him apart."

Apparently that is what I do in round two, which is over before I can think about it. I must have been on autopilot, because the bell is ringing again, and I'm walking back to the stool again. As I look back over my shoulder, I notice that Tipper is limping as he walks. I vaguely remember having a leg lock on him right after I got knocked down by whatever it was that hit me in my right temple and left this lump there that Jao is icing.

"Even fight," Jao says. "Win it in the final round."

The bell rings again. As we meet at the center of the

ring, Tipper is the first one to extend his gloves for us to tap at the start of this final round.

Think he respects you now? my inner voice asks.

I don't have time to think back an answer. After stepping back, Tipper has just shown his respect in the form of a superhard roundhouse toward my temple. I just manage to block with a right forearm, and I bounce back against the rope. My arm feels numb. I wonder if it's broken. Might be. But my left arm reaches up as Tipper closes with me. I hook my hand around his neck and kick at his inner knee with my opposite leg. Tipper goes down, me on top of him this time. We transition from one move to another. Him on top, then me again. If my arm wasn't hurting so much, it'd be one of the better rolls I've ever executed. As it is, I'm not sure how long I can keep this up.

There's just one last thing to try. My long legs lock around his body. Somehow I'm on his back, and my good arm is around his neck. It hurts, but I manage to reach up with my bad arm and lock my hand over the top of his head, my other hand over my right bicep. And squeeze.

He's ready to tap out. I can feel it. But the bell rings, and I relax my hold. Tipper rolls over, then looks down at me, still on my back. This time he reaches out a hand. As he pulls me to my feet, he leans close.

"Great fight, Spider."

"Thanks," I say.

And as we wait together for the judges, I know that whatever the decision might be, I've won.

THE TROPHY
BY GORDON KORMAN

Every time Lucas closes his eyes, the scene plays out like a YouTube video imprinted on his brain waves:

Shimmy gets the ball in the corner, down by a point. Four seconds left on the clock. There's a defender in his face. No way can a four-foot-eleven point guard shoot over him. Shimmy's trapped. Three seconds now . . . There it is, the trademark shimmy! He head-fakes to the left while moving to the right. A gasp threatens to suck all the air out of the gym as his high-top comes down millimeters—*no, what's smaller than millimeters?*—from the out-of-bounds line. The silence of the referee's whistle *not* blowing is the loudest sound Lucas can remember.

Two seconds. Shimmy's pass is on its way. Lucas snatches

it out of the air at the top of the key. He charges into the paint. A big body blocks his way, appearing as if by black magic.

Wham! Collision. But—no foul. The ref is going to let this play out.

One second left. A game clock loaded with twenty-four hundred heartbeats has run down to this ultimate tick. Defenders can be beaten, but not time itself. No chance to put the ball on the floor, no move to the left or right. There's only one option, one *direction*—

Up.

Lucas isn't much of a leaper, but in that instant, his legs are superpowered by the screams of the crowd and all the desperation of the final second of the championship game. He springs, feeling the air beneath him—more air than he can ever recall before. The ball leaves his hands a split second before the buzzer sounds. He's so panicked by the prospect of a block that he gets off a clumsy shot with an awkward high trajectory. The defender swipes at it, fingertips passing barely a half inch below.

Lucas waits for the swish, *prays* for it. . . .

The clunk of the ball against the back of the rim resounds like a bomb blast. The shot ricochets high—weirdly high. For an instant, it's frozen there, level with the top of the backboard. Then it drops like a stone through the hoop, snapping the net.

Final score: 43–42 for the Hollow Log Middle School Hammers, city champions.

Pandemonium.

At this point, Lucas's vision begins to blur. The team is in a raucous, disorganized huddle, bouncing up and down as ecstatic spectators rush the floor. Kids are actually crying—or is that the parents? Maybe it's Coach Skillicorn who's crying—this is his first championship in twenty-seven years of coaching.

One memory that's crystal clear is the trophy: the Interboro Cup. Four gleaming Winged Victory figures holding up a golden basketball. The only thing more beautiful than the cup itself is what it represents. Thirty-two sixth-grade teams enter the tournament; one gets to hoist this prize. Not their finals opponent, the Sunnyside Heat, top seeds at the start of the competition. Not even the five-time champion Revere Raiders, the city's perennial powerhouse.

Us.

Even now, weeks later, as Lucas and Shimmy pass the gym on the way to their lockers, they always glance to the left, treating their eyes to the sight of . . .

The pair freezes. The display case stands open. The Interboro Cup is nowhere to be seen.

"Where's the trophy?" Shimmy demands.

"Relax," says Lucas. "There could be a million totally normal reasons why it isn't there."

"Like what?"

"Like they sent it out to be polished. Or engraved. Maybe we're going to get our names on it."

Shimmy is unimpressed. His real name is James Tracey Abandando. James = Jimmy = Shimmy.

At that moment, Coach Skillicorn steps out of the athletic office. The boys can see right away that something is wrong. Coach has been a changed man since the big win: taller, confident. Now he seems changed back again: hunched, nervous, gray in the face. He gestures to the display case. "Do you two know anything about this?"

"You mean the trophy?" Lucas asks. "It's missing? Are you sure someone didn't just take it out to shine it up or something?"

Coach shakes his head sadly. "The lock has been picked. It's a theft. No question about it."

Lucas is bewildered. "But who would want to steal our trophy?"

Shimmy stares at him. "What are you talking about,

man? It's the trophy! It's the most valuable thing in our school!"

"It's valuable to us because we won it," Lucas insists. "To anybody else it's just a metal statue on a block of wood." He turns to the coach. "What do the police say?"

"We haven't called them yet," Skillicorn replies. "Principal Updike thinks it's just a prank pulled by somebody here." He sighs. "I hope he's right."

Sure enough, right at the beginning of homeroom, Dr. Updike comes on the PA system: *"Attention, students. Someone has removed the Interboro Cup from the display case outside the gymnasium. To that person, I say perhaps you thought this was a fine joke, but I'll have you know that the rest of us are not amused. We are all very proud of our sixth-grade basketball team, which has reached a level of excellence never before achieved in the history of Hollow Log Middle School. You have until the end of the day to return the trophy to its place, and no names will be taken and no questions asked. I trust you to do the right thing."*

Shimmy leans over to Lucas. "You know, Updike may have a PhD, but he sure isn't very smart. If you went to all the trouble to swipe the greatest trophy in the history of the world, would you give it back just because some principal says you won't get in trouble?"

"I'll bet it was one of the eighth graders," grumbles Obert Marcus—power forward—known as O-Mark on the team. "Those guys think they rule the school. They can't stand anybody else getting attention."

Shimmy stays on message. "They have to call the cops. Only police have the power to break into lockers and search the whole building."

"No matter what happens to the cup," Lucas tells them, "we're still champions. No one can take that away from us."

Shimmy isn't buying it. "And how do you prove that to people? By showing them your trophy!"

As the day progresses, Lucas, Shimmy, and all the Hammers find reason after reason to stop by the gym and keep an eye on the display case. The space where the trophy sat yawns a little wider every time.

"The trophy's just a symbol," Lucas repeats. But he's lying, even to himself, and everybody knows it. The kid who hit the winning shot wants the Interboro Cup back more than any of them—except possibly Coach Skillicorn, who has left school early due to "a migraine." By the 3:30 bell, Coach has sent his team members six text messages encouraging them not to despair. Each one sounds more despairing than the last.

Lucas passes by the gym on his way out of the building. The case is still empty.

When Lucas picks up the phone, Max Tehrani—shooting guard and team captain—is on the other end. "You'd better see this. Get over here."

By the time he makes it to Max's, the whole team is there, crowded around the Tehranis' computer. He catches a tragic look from Shimmy, but before he can ask, the captain begins his explanation.

"When I got back from school, *this* was posted on my Facebook wall." Max pounds the keyboard, and the image grows until it's practically full-screen.

The boys stare. The picture is distorted by blurry patches, but there's no question that they're looking at four Winged Victory figures hoisting a golden ball: the Interboro Cup.

"Our trophy!" Shimmy exclaims in anguish.

The photograph is a close-up, with the pedestal of the cup out of view, so it's impossible to see what the base is resting on. A dark, indistinct form runs across the top of the frame.

"It's under some kind of roof," Lucas observes.

"Or an awning," Max agrees. "And that pole in the background could be a support for it."

A four-word message accompanies the picture in block capital letters.

COME AND GET ME!!!!

"Come and get me *where*?" Shimmy shouts.

Jeff Leventhal—small forward—has a practical question. "Who took the picture? Find the sender, and you've found the trophy."

Max shakes his head sadly and scrolls to the far margin. Under "posted by" is:

4u2findout.

"Cute," mumbles O-Mark.

"It's not cute." Shimmy moans in true pain. "Don't you get it? This is like a ransom note! It's like saying: 'We have the Interboro Cup. If you ever want to see it again, put a million dollars in a Walgreens bag and drop it in the trash can at Seventy-first and Kissena.'"

"It doesn't mention anything about money," Jeff reminds him. "It just says 'Come and get me.'"

Lucas is still peering at the screen as if trying to will a set of GPS coordinates to appear at the top of the photograph. "Wait a minute. What's all this stuff in the background?"

Max, who's good with computers, sections off a square from the top right corner of the picture and blows it up. Frowning, he imports the image to a photo-enhancement program. As he skillfully clicks on various controls, the picture gradually becomes more distinct.

Shimmy is bewildered. "It's just a row of stores."

"No," Lucas amends. "It's a row of stores behind the spot where they stashed our trophy." His eyes fall on a dark sign with orange lettering:

EPIC JERK
Caribbean Restaurant

"Google it!"

A moment later, the address is on the screen: 224A Sterling Avenue, West Hook.

"That has to be the place," he decides. "No way are there two restaurants in town called Epic Jerk."

"So what happens now?" O-Mark asks. "We call Coach, and he goes to the cops?"

Lucas shakes his head. "No cops. No adults, period. By the time they're done making inquiries, whoever took the cup will move it to the toilet tank in his subbasement. It's our trophy; we have to get it ourselves."

"West Hook is all the way on the other side of town!" Jeff protests.

"There's such a thing as buses, you know," says Shimmy. "Nobody's going to make you travel by pogo stick."

Max has a practical concern. "Even if we can get to the restaurant, that doesn't mean we'll be able to find the trophy from there. Come to think of it, there's no guarantee that the trophy's still in the spot where the picture was taken."

Lucas takes a deep breath. "I know. But right now it's all we've got to go on."

The trophy is just a symbol . . .

They're his own words, but Lucas struggles to believe them. Sure, the Interboro Cup isn't what makes them champions. Its absence from the case outside the gym doesn't change what happened in the sixth-grade tournament.

You don't cross the city on two buses and a subway for a symbol—not even the symbol of the greatest thing you've ever done.

And that doesn't even take into account how *weird* all this is. Who kidnaps a trophy? He knows he's letting his imagination get the better of him, yet heading off into the total unknown undoubtedly carries a certain amount of danger. Surely the guys see that too. Why else the reluctance of some of them to go along with this?

He shakes his head. No trophy can make you a champion. But what champion won't man up and take back his prize?

There's a decent turnout at the bus stop. The starting five—Lucas, Shimmy, O-Mark, Jeff, and Max—plus Dalton Chen, the shrimp of the team, but with a scorching outside jump shot. Also—Lucas's eyes fall on a tiny red-haired girl hugging a ratty plush bunny that's been through countless laundry cycles. The kid is Ariella, Max's six-year-old sister.

Lucas nudges Max. "What's she doing here?"

The Hammers' captain shrugs miserably. "My parents both work Saturdays. I have to babysit, no getting out of it."

"Yeah, but does she need to bring the toy?" Shimmy asks in annoyance.

"Mr. Fluffernutter is *not* a toy; he's an elderly rabbit gentleman," Ariella says defiantly.

"I'm stuck," Max explains. "If I make her leave the rodent, she'll rat me out to our folks. I assume I'm not the only one who wasn't totally honest about what we're doing today."

A chorus of nods greets this announcement, along with an accounting of the various excuses, half-truths, white lies, and outright whoppers the boys cooked up to explain what will surely be an errand that takes a good chunk of the day.

At last, the bus pulls up to the curb and the Hollow Log Hammers file aboard, sister and Mr. Fluffernutter in tow.

On the ride to the subway station, Shimmy brings up the question that's on everybody's lips. "Do you think we're going to run into the low-down sleazoid who ripped off our trophy?"

"We have to be ready for anything," Lucas replies. "Remember the Facebook message—it said 'Come and get me.' If that's not a challenge, I don't know what is."

"But we don't know anybody in West Hook," Jeff puts in. "And why would anybody in West Hook know us?"

"The tournament covers the whole city," Dalton points out. "Could these be the guys we beat in the final?"

Max shakes his head. "That team was from Sunnyside."

"Maybe they stole the trophy and took it over to West Hook just to mess with our heads," Shimmy suggests.

Lucas looks impatient. "It doesn't matter. We'll find out when we get there, and we'll deal with whatever we have to."

"Are we there yet?" Ariella whines. "Mr. Fluffernutter

wants to go home." Which means Ariella wants to go home.

"Mr. Fluffernutter is in for a long day," her brother tells her.

They get off the bus at the subway station and descend two long staircases to the trains. The westbound platform is wall-to-wall people. It's a physical effort for the teammates to stay together. Max keeps an iron grip on his sister's arm.

"You're hurting Mr. Fluffernutter," she complains.

"He'll get over it," Max growls. "He's a rabbit, for crying out loud."

The train is even more packed than the station. Lucas can't reach a pole or a handle. But it's okay, because it's impossible to fall when you're packed in like a sardine. The other Hammers are similarly squashed at various places around the car.

As they clatter through the darkness of the tunnel, Lucas concentrates on the station names. The last thing they want to do is miss their stop. He's trying to decipher the subway map, when, out of the corner of his eye, he spies a white rabbit exiting the train attached to the Velcro strap on a man's cell phone pouch.

A shriek cuts the air. *"Mr. Fluffernutter!!!"*

Ariella snakes across the car and out the door in pursuit of her beloved toy.

"Ariella! Come back!" Max is struggling to follow, but he's too hemmed in. He's not going to make it.

The tone sounds. The doors begin to close.

"Awwww—" Lucas jams his way through and hits the platform running. At a level of athleticism that matches his moves on his winning basket, he grabs Ariella with one hand and, with the other, snatches the rabbit off the man's strap. Then he wheels on a dime and sprints back for the car.

Too late.

The last thing Lucas sees as the train moves on into the tunnel is the terrified faces of his teammates pressed against the windows, staring out at him through the smeared glass.

Shimmy holds his hand over the mouthpiece of his cell phone. "It's okay. They're on the next train. They'll be here any minute."

The sighs of relief move the air. The five remaining Hammers sit in the back of the T-19 bus, which is parked in the station, waiting to begin its route to West Hook. Max's sigh is the biggest of all. Recovering the trophy is optional; recovering Ariella is mandatory.

"Did they rescue Mr. Fluffernutter?" Dalton asks anxiously.

"What do you care?" Shimmy explodes. "He's the reason we're in this whole mess! He's a rabbit—and he isn't even a *real* rabbit!"

"Look!" O-Mark exclaims, pointing back at the station. "Here they come!"

Out of the darkness, a larger figure, a smaller one, and a bouncing white blob are running full tilt for the bus.

"They made it!" Max cheers.

No sooner have the words passed his lips than the doors close, the gears grind, and the bus is moving off down the street.

"Wait!" Shimmy howls. "Our friends are back there!"

"Got a schedule, kid," the driver tosses over his shoulder. "If I'm late, it's a mark against me."

No amount of begging or pleading makes any difference.

The group passes the trip in silence. The sole exception is Shimmy, who updates his teammates on the increasingly agitated text messages from Lucas back at the station, waiting for the next T-19 bus. The others have their eyes out the window, watching for Sterling Avenue. West Hook is a lot older than their part of town, the ancient, fading signs difficult to read.

Suddenly, Jeff is on his feet, pointing and shouting.

"Look—it's the restaurant! From the Facebook picture!"

Max squints at the orange lettering. Epic Jerk. He pulls the cord, and the five Hammers get off. There's an awkward moment as they stand on the corner, watching the bus drive away. The triumph of reaching their destination fades quickly. Finding the restaurant and finding the trophy are two different matters. All they know for certain is that Epic Jerk is visible from wherever the trophy was when the photograph was taken.

"So," rumbles O-Mark in his deep voice, "what happens now?"

Max looks thoughtful. "For the restaurant to show up in the background, the trophy would have to be"—he swings around to face the park across the street—"there."

It's a smallish square taking up six city blocks, with pathways and benches organized around a central fountain.

"Remember the picture," Dalton advises. "There was a roof, or some kind of cover, with a support pole in back."

"We'll scour the place," Max decides. "Every inch. If our trophy's here, we'll find it."

In a third-floor apartment on Sterling Avenue, a very large twelve-year-old boy gazes out his window at the park below. He picks up a cell phone and speed-dials a number.

"Yeah?" comes a sharp, piercing voice.

"They're here," says the boy.

"Really? Are you sure?"

He squints down through the glass, watching the Hollow Log Hammers exploring the square. "Get the gang together. It's time."

"What do you mean, it isn't there?" Lucas rasps into the handset, racing along Sterling Avenue, dragging Ariella by the hand.

"Mr. Fluffernutter can't go any farther," the little girl complains.

"We searched the whole park," comes Shimmy's voice over the phone. "We even went through the bushes. They must've moved the trophy after they took the picture. Where are you, man? We've been here, like, forever!"

"We missed our bus," Lucas replies savagely, "because Mr. Fluffernutter had to go to the bathroom—"

"He's only human," Ariella sulks.

"—so we ran like crazy, but the bus we got on turned out to be a T-*18* not a T-19—wait! I think I see you guys!" Squeezing the girl's wrist, which makes her cry out, Lucas turns on the jets. They sprint past Epic Jerk and into the park to their companions.

Overcome with relief, Max enfolds his sister in a bear hug. She pulls back and boots him savagely in the shin.

"*Ow!* What was that for?"

"You're supposed to take care of me!" she rages. "If I get lost, where does that leave Mr. Fluffernutter?"

"He was lost *with* you!" Max tries to defend himself.

Shimmy approaches Lucas. "What are we going to do, man? There's no trophy here. I'm starting to think we came all this way for nothing!"

Lucas looks desperately around the square. There are not a lot of potential hiding places. It's a small park, with a kids' playground, a basketball court, a dog run, and a handful of paved paths and benches arranged around a huge fountain in the middle. At the center of the fountain, atop a granite pedestal, is a wrought iron sculpture of two young children huddled under an umbrella. The "rain" is provided by a ring of jets around the circumference.

"Wait a minute . . . Guys—" Lucas points. The pieces are starting to fit together. In the Facebook photograph, the roof is actually the umbrella; the pole is its handle. The blurry spots are caused by the cascading water. And, far in the background, the clue that brought them here—Epic Jerk.

They all look, and catch a glint of gold.

There, balanced on the spot where the figures' hands come together, sits the Interboro Cup.

"Our trophy!" exclaims Shimmy, leading the stampede to the fountain.

"Yeah, but how are we going to get it?" Jeff wonders. A lot of water stands between them and the cup. "We'll drown!"

Lucas doesn't care. He kicks off his shoes and socks, rolls up his pants, and steps over the edge, disappearing almost to the knees in the cold, clammy pool. The chill makes him laugh with sheer delight. "Come on, guys. What's a little water compared with the blood and sweat that went into winning this thing?"

Footwear flies, and all six Hammers are in the fountain in less than thirty seconds.

"Boys are crazy," says Ariella from the sideline. "Oh, I don't mean *you*, Mr. Fluffernutter. You're not a boy; you're an elderly rabbit gentleman."

Rescuing the trophy turns out to be a major operation. Max and Lucas form the base of the pyramid, with Shimmy on their shoulders. He, in turn, boosts Dalton to the top of the pedestal. There are a few scary moments since the polished stone is wet and slippery. But soon the whooping Hollow Log Hammers are splashing their way out of the fountain in a flurry of dripping high fives, sur-rounding Max, their triumphant captain, who holds their trophy aloft in the brilliant sky. It's a good thing the spring weather is warm or their next stop would be the hospital, to treat six cases of hypothermia. They are drenched yet jubilant. The Interboro Cup is once again with its owners, and all's right with the world.

"Let's get back to the bus stop," Shimmy exhorts his teammates. "The sooner we blow this Popsicle stand and get home, the better."

"Not so fast" comes a deep voice.

For the first time, the Hammers look around. Seven boys have appeared almost out of nowhere and now stand facing them. They don't seem threatening. But they don't look friendly, either.

Lucas puts two and two together. "You're the guys who stole our trophy!"

A sandy-haired boy who's almost a single extended freckle nods solemnly. "Or maybe you're the guys who stole *our* trophy," he says in a high-pitched, piercing tone.

Shimmy bristles. "What's that supposed to mean?"

"We're the Revere Raiders—" Freckle begins.

Light dawns on Lucas. Revere Middle School is a city powerhouse in basketball. In the tournament, it was a major relief when the Raiders were eliminated in the semifinal by Sunnyside, the Hammers' opponent in the championship game. "So how's it your trophy?" he asks. "You guys got knocked out."

A huge kid, at least a head taller than Lucas, pipes up, "We got shafted."

Freckle explains. "Meet Igor, best sixth grader in the city. We would have crushed Sunnyside with him."

"So why didn't you?" O-Mark growls.

"Academically ineligible," mourns Igor in a voice even deeper than O-Mark's rumble. "Got an incomplete in Social Studies."

"That's your problem," Shimmy accuses. "Staying eligible's part of the game."

"Had mono last semester," the big boy admits sadly. "My teacher wouldn't cut me any slack."

Lucas's anger evaporates in an instant. Winning the tournament was the greatest feeling ever. To be robbed of a shot at that by a tough break had to hurt.

Even Shimmy finds some sympathy for the Raiders. "Man, that's rough."

There's general agreement among the Hammers. "But why blame us?" Max asks. "We didn't flunk Igor; his teacher did."

"We're not blaming you," Freckle explains. "You won; we accept that. But we weren't in that tournament—not the *real* us."

"What are you trying to say?" Lucas demands.

Freckle shrugs. "Well—we're here, and you're here, and the trophy's here. . . ."

It isn't a fair fight, and the boys from Hollow Log know it. First of all, neither team has its full complement of players. Second, the Hammers are soaked to the skin and exhausted from the adventures of the day. And third—

"Why should we have to play a bunch of trophy-stealers to win the trophy we already won?" Shimmy complains.

"The trophy's not important—" Lucas begins.

"That's not what you said when you made us wade through Niagara Falls to get it," Jeff puts in sourly.

"The Raiders have a point," insists Lucas.

"They're not exactly Boy Scouts, you know," Max observes. "They crossed the whole city, walked into Hollow Log, and walked out with the Interboro Cup."

Lucas holds up his hands. "Listen—what does that trophy mean if we only won because that Igor kid couldn't play? Is that the kind of champions you want to be: a team that only made good because of somebody else's rotten luck?"

"I can't jump in wet jeans," Dalton complains.

Shimmy smiles in spite of himself. "You can't jump, period. It never stopped you before."

Jeff asks the question that's on everyone's mind. "What if we *lose*?"

"We won't," Lucas says confidently. "We're the Hollow Log Hammers. We rocked the tournament, and we'll rock West Hook too."

The court is concrete instead of hardwood. The nets are made of chain not mesh, so a swish sounds more like a clank. There are no referees and only three substitutes between the two teams. The audience consists of a six-year-old girl and a stuffed rabbit. The Interboro Cup stands by the out-of-bounds line, as if watching the contest that will decide its fate.

It's on.

The Raiders run off the first three baskets, but Hollow Log recovers quickly, closing the gap to two points. The teams are evenly matched, with Igor's bulk controlling the middle but Dalton's outside jumpers keeping the Hammers close. Shimmy uses his quickness to slice through Revere's zone defense, and soon the Hammers have a narrow lead. Lucas can't shoot over Igor but finally manages to submarine past the big boy and lay the ball in off the backboard.

Another Raider sinks back-to-back ten footers, and the teams are tied at 16.

Freckle is impressed. "Maybe you chumps really *are* champs!"

"Sunnyside was lucky to get past you guys," Lucas admits, panting.

"Mr. Fluffernutter's bored" is the audience's opinion.

By this time, the Hammers have forgotten their bus woes and wet clothes. They haven't faced this kind of competition since the championship game. Revere pulls ahead, but Hollow Log roars back, scoring on five straight possessions. A heated argument over an alleged foul evaporates when O-Mark knocks down the longest jump shot any of them has ever seen. Not to be outdone, big Igor rips the ball out of Jeff's hands and comes amazingly close to dunking it—another vertical inch or two is all he would have needed. By now they've been playing for a solid hour, the score knotted at 36 . . . or is it 38?

A light rain begins, waking Ariella, who's fallen asleep on a bench using her stuffed toy as a pillow. The Raiders and Hammers are just getting started. A second hour falls away like nothing. Hollow Log leads, 74–72 . . . or maybe 72–70. But a disputed basket from about half an hour ago means it's possible the two teams are actually tied again. It's hard to keep track of the score, Lucas reflects, when the action is so intense; when you're running your hardest, and jumping your highest, and every gasping breath comes out of your lungs in a ball of fire; when you're having this much fun.

They are well into their third hour when both teams' cell phones begin ringing. Soon their game is being set to music amid a chorus of electronic tones. The boys ignore it as long as they can, but it's starting to get dark . . .

Suddenly, Shimmy points. "The bus!"

No one wants to leave. But if you miss a bus on a Saturday night, who knows when the next one will be along?

The Hammers grab Ariella and Mr. Fluffernutter and fly—but not before Lucas and Freckle exchange numbers on their phones. This game isn't over yet! And besides, nobody remembers the score. . . .

Whatever. They'll settle it next week on Hollow Log's home turf.

Lucas can hardly wait.

Shimmy slaps him a high five as they take their seats. "That was awesome! Man, we're some beasts to keep up with those guys!"

There is general agreement, except from Ariella. "Mr. Fluffernutter's *telling*!" she promises her brother.

Max is flushed with a mix of exhaustion and happiness.

"Go ahead. I don't care. Today was worth getting in trouble!"

The bus pulls away. The Hammers peer out the window, watching their new friends and rivals heading for home.

In the shadowy darkness of the park, a lone object stands at the edge of the court, utterly forgotten. Its shape is four Winged Victory figures holding up a golden basketball.

I WILL DESTROY YOU, DEREK JETER

BY CHRIS RYLANDER

"Derek Jeter must die," I announced.

"Uh, Wes, don't you think that's a little extreme?" Nate said as he struggled to get his backpack off his shoulder without letting it smash against his right arm.

I stood up from our table in the school cafeteria and paced back and forth next to my seat. I considered what Derek Jeter had done to me, and also to Nate for that matter, his arm in a cast and sling. Then I thought about Jeter's stupid smiling face after he got base hits that drove in runs and won games, and how he was able to go on with his life as if nothing at all had happened.

In case you don't know who Derek Jeter is, which is

unlikely, he is the All-Star shortstop for the New York Yankees, five-time World Series champion, former Rookie of the Year, beloved hero to pretty much all Yankees fans worldwide, the most liked and praised baseball player in the whole league for almost twenty years, and also likely the most overrated jerk ever to hold a baseball bat.

"Hey, catch!" someone called out.

An eighth grader, walking by with his group of friends, tossed me his pint of milk. It caught me by surprise and, despite my best efforts, bobbled around in my clumsy hands for a couple seconds before landing on the floor with a splat.

The kid and his group of friends laughed. And when other kids nearby saw it was me who had dropped the milk, they all laughed, too.

"Nice catch, butterfingers!" some kid yelled. "Someone check the internet, Jacoby Ellsbury might have just gotten his leg shattered."

This was followed by more laughter, of course.

I sighed and sat back down. I looked at Nate. He was fidgeting with the top bun of his chicken patty sandwich with his lone functioning arm, trying to simultaneously pretend that he was just there by accident, that he wasn't really my friend, and that that whole incident hadn't actually happened. Like he always did.

"No," I said to him.

"Huh?" Nate asked, barely able to make eye contact.

"You asked me if what I said was a little extreme. My answer is no. In fact, it's not extreme enough if you want my honest answer. Derek Jeter must die!"

"Yeah, but you don't really want him dead-dead, do you? I mean, that's . . ."

"No, of course not," I admitted. "But I am going to kill his career, ruin his reputation just like he ruined mine. Mark my words: Derek Jeter is going to pay." Then I looked north in the general direction of the Bronx and said, while clenching my hand into a fist, "I will destroy you, Derek Jeter."

The place smelled like stale cinnamon and boiled hot dogs. If I didn't need help so badly, I probably would have turned and left right away. But as it was, curses aren't something you can just give to people as easy as handing them a dollar. A trained professional was needed for these things.

"Hey, kid, do you have an appointment?" A man was sitting on a single chair in the middle of the room. He was wearing a white T-shirt with no sleeves that said THIS IS WHAT A COOL GRANDPA LOOKS LIKE, even though he was only, like, thirty years old. Also, he was greasy, like he wouldn't have been out of place at all in some diner's kitchen, flipping over giant piles of hash browns. To be honest, he wasn't really what I'd expected.

Then again, I'd never been to a witch doctor before, so I didn't really know what I'd expected.

The witch doctor stood up as we approached and then saw Nick's cast and sling and shook his head. "Hey, I'm not that kind of doctor, you know."

"Yeah, I know," I said, handing him a printed copy of the confirmation email he'd sent me. "We have an appointment."

He peered at it for a while as if he'd never seen it before.

The witch doctor went by the name Doctor Zanzubu Zardoz, according to his website. He had pretty good references and everything. Well, if you can count a couple of online reviews posted by people with handles like "spcehed111" and "nachosnachosnachos" and "tUbEmOn-KeYgOaT" as good references, that is. And I tend to think you can.

I'd gotten the idea from the years of suffering for Red Sox fans I'd heard my grandpa complain about every Thanksgiving. The Boston Red Sox, who have been my family's favorite team going way back to, like, my grandpa's grandpa or something, had this curse on them for a really long time. The Curse of the Bambino.

Basically, this curse began the day the Sox sold Babe Ruth to the Yankees back in 1920. And for almost one hundred years, the Red Sox didn't win a single World Series. Some Red Sox fans, like my great-grandpa, lived their whole life and died without ever getting to see them win a championship. But then this dude named Theo Epstein came along and became their general manager and broke the curse, and the Red Sox finally won a World Series in 2004.

Apparently, the Chicago Cubs have an even worse curse on their team. They haven't won it at all since 1908! And it's pretty much proven to be the result of something called the Curse of the Billy Goat. They still haven't figured out how to break it. They stole away the Red Sox curse breaker, General Manager Theo Epstein, but even he hasn't been able to crack that one yet.

Anyway, that's where I got the idea to go to a witch doctor. I saw on some message board that secretly that's how Theo was able to break the Curse of the Bambino. Some people say it was through good farm-system development, others claim it was a series of good trades, and most believe it was a combination of those two things plus truckloads of money used to buy up all the best free agents. But I found out the truth from this dude online who goes by the name BucknerMustDie86. He said his brother's neighbor's gardener's cousin's best friend's wife's masseuse's former T-ball coach's nephew's mailman's sister's ex-boyfriend's mechanic was old college roommates with Theo and that Theo Epstein actually visited a witch doctor at the start of the 2004 season. And that proof of this could be seen when the Red Sox came back to win from being down 0–3 in the Division Series against the Yankees, something no other team has ever done before or since in baseball's 150-year history.

So I figured if a witch doctor can break a curse that powerful, then surely he could make a curse that powerful, too.

"Basic curses are fifty, and hexes are thirty-five. Payment up front," Doctor Zanzubu Zardoz said.

"I want the full fifty." I handed him the credit card I'd borrowed from Nate's dad's wallet the night before. His dad had dozens of credit cards for some reason, so he'd never even notice.

"Is this really your card?" he asked. "You look a little young."

"Of course it is," I said.

Of course we both knew it wasn't. I mean, I was twelve.

And I didn't even look old for my age. And Nate looked even younger than I did. But at the same time, if the witch doctor called me out, then he wouldn't get paid.

A short time later, after Doctor Zanzubu Zardoz had run the card and put on a hat that looked and smelled like it was made out of old KFC chicken bones, we went through a small door back into his "office."

"Do you have an object that belongs to the subject?" he asked.

"Uh, I have this," I said, and handed him the autographed picture of Derek Jeter that I'd gotten the day after he ruined my life.

Doctor Zanzubu Zardoz looked at the picture and was barely able to hide a grin.

"Close enough," he said. "What do you want done? What are the specifics of your curse?"

"I want him to go into an epic slump," I said. "I mean, like the sort of thing that forces him into retirement. I'm talking below-the-Mendoza-Line bad. I don't even want him on the Interstate by the end of it; I want him way below that. Make him go one for his next eighty-seven at bats. No, one for the next hundred and eighty-seven! And throw in seventeen errors while you're at it. I want him to cause the Yankees to lose every game in September and miss the play-offs. I want people to see him for the washed-up old hack he really is instead of some sort of treasured national hero. Send him into retirement where he belongs."

"Jeez, kid," Doctor Zanzubu Zardoz said. "Well, I guess you're lucky I'm a Mets fan."

Then he started chanting something in a language I thought I recognized as Klingon from *Star Trek*. I exchanged a glance with Nate, who made a face like he wanted me to call out Doctor Zanzubu Zardoz as some sort of fraud. But I didn't. If I did, there'd be no curse.

The doctor finished chanting after a few minutes and then tossed some old chicken bones, a few feathers, and what looked like red hotels from the board game Monopoly into a wooden bowl. He set it on top of the autographed picture of Derek Jeter and said one final Klingon phrase.

"Okay, kid, you're good to go," he said.

"That's it?"

"That's it."

"So, like, when will his slump start?" I asked. "Tonight?"

"Sure." Doctor ZZ handed me my picture and showed us to the exit.

That night, Derek Jeter went 4 for 4 with two home runs, a double, and seven RBIs. And Boston's supposed ace, Jon

Lester, had been the starting pitcher. And Jeter supposedly had the flu that night, which had those saps at ESPN
praising him even more than they already would have. I
bet they have a whole room that serves only as a shrine to
Derek Jeter at ESPN headquarters, and all the employees
change into Yankee pinstripe uniforms and Derek Jeter
masks and go in there once a day to light candles and sing
the seventh-inning stretch song.

"I don't get it," I said to Nate the next day at lunch. "The
curse was supposed to start last night!"

"Where did you find that witch doctor guy again?" he
asked.

"The internet, remember?" I said.

"Oh, yeah . . ."

"Maybe it will start tonight?" I suggested, ignoring his
cynical tone. When you've only got one friend left in the
world, you have to make such oversights sometimes.

"Maybe," Nate said, but I could tell he clearly didn't
think so.

And Nate was right, of course. Over the next several
weeks, Jeter went on a hot streak of historic proportions.
He hit an astounding .562 with seven home runs, eleven
stolen bases, and nineteen RBIs. It was the best eleven-
game stretch of his career. Maybe of anybody's career, ever.

There was even talk now on ESPN that Jeter might be in the running for MVP since he was doing all his damage in September, when it mattered the most considering the Yankees were right in the middle of the play-off race like always. If he did win, he'd be the oldest MVP in baseball history. As if he needed another record or more reason to be worshipped.

At one point, this guy on ESPN—a skinny, bald dude with three names—actually drooled all over his tie when he was showing highlights of Jeter hitting for the cycle. Which, yeah, he did hit for the cycle a few days after the curse supposedly started. I would have asked for a refund from Doctor Zanzubu Zardoz, but it wasn't my money, and he'd already done enough damage as it was.

To make matters worse, somehow Nate's dad did notice the charge on his credit card bill a few days after we'd placed the curse. Apparently, Nate got yelled at pretty bad and grounded for several weeks. And his dad took away his TV, which had to really stink since that was pretty much Nate's only source of fun anymore with the broken elbow and being grounded and all.

But what mattered even more than all of that was that the failed curse meant I'd need to take this to the next level if I really wanted to get my revenge on Derek Jeter.

*   *   *

So, you may be wondering just what exactly had Derek Jeter done to me to deserve this kind of wrath? Well, I'll tell you.

It was my birthday, and my favorite team, the Boston Red Sox, were in town for an important late-August four-game series with the Yankees. My dad had been lucky enough to score us some amazing seats about eight rows back, right off of third base. It was perfect; I'd get to see the Red Sox pulverize the Yankees in Yankee Stadium on my birthday with my dad and best friend, Nate.

And it was the night before my seventh-grade class voted on class president. The most recent polls showed that I was all but guaranteed to win. As class president, my popularity would get a major boost. I had already prepared my acceptance speech.

And to top everything off, Sara Hernandez, who I'd had a crush on since first grade, was sitting just a few rows behind us. As we sat down, she smiled and gave me a little presidential salute.

Basically, my life couldn't have been more perfect that night.

Until the fifth inning, that is.

That's when Jeter came up to bat for his third plate

appearance. The score was 4–2; Boston was winning. Jeter was hitless so far. He fell behind in the count quickly, no balls and two strikes looking. Then the old, desperate man that he is, he just started swinging at everything. He fouled off four straight pitches. I was screaming at Lester to throw him a curveball or two. Or at least throw him something off the plate.

But he didn't. Instead, he threw more fastballs, each just on the edge of the strike zone. Jeter fouled off one. He fouled off another. And then, on the third, he hit a towering foul pop-up that started drifting toward our seats. I quickly pulled out my glove. I'd been to several games before, but I'd yet to ever get a ball.

It was so high that I lost it for several seconds. But suddenly I had it again and realized it was coming right at me. I had it. I really did. I don't even know what happened next, honestly, because I had that thing in my sights, I'm telling you. It was all but in my glove.

But as the replay showed again and again and again and again and again, I clearly didn't have it. In fact, what happened was that, right after I nudged Nate out of my way so I could make the catch cleanly, I ended up missing the ball entirely, and it nailed me right in the face.

The blow sent me reeling backward, and my limbs

flailed wildly. The chain reaction of events that I started in that one moment is almost too ridiculous to believe. In fact, if it wasn't well documented by numerous TV cameras, I wouldn't believe it had actually happened the way it did at all.

Anyway, first Nate tried to grab me to keep me from tumbling back into the seats behind me. But he wasn't able to stop my momentum, and we both ended up spilling over our seats back into the row behind us. As we fell, I accidently knocked a guy's full tray of nachos up in the air and spilled two full sodas all over two little kids, who promptly started bawling. The nachos landed on the team president's wife's head. (Yeah, about that, what was the team president doing down in the stands and not in a luxury box anyway? I guess he was trying to seem more like a regular fan instead of some big-shot rich executive, which is exactly what he was.)

When the nachos hit her head, the hot cheese sauce caused her to launch her full soda backward, where it splashed all over Sara Hernandez. She got a face and lap full of Coke and ice, likely ruining my chances of ever getting to even speak to her again without her punching me in the temple repeatedly.

Then Sara spilled her soda on an old guy in the aisle

next to her. He was holding two sodas at the time himself, both of which proceeded to spill as well. It was like a rousing game of sodinoes (soda + dominoes). One soda ended up in the lap of an old war veteran who started having some sort of war flashback and spilled several more drinks on several other important people while air machine gunning everybody around him before diving across two rows of seats onto an imaginary live grenade. I guess if there's one thing I learned that night besides the fact that Derek Jeter is an even bigger jerk than I'd always thought, it's that the only people who can afford the good seats at Yankee stadium are generally pretty important people. And also that spilling beverages on old war veterans can be hazardous to your health.

Anyway, the second soda landed on the steps where a pretty heavy guy holding a huge tray of food just happened to be walking by. He slipped and went tumbling down the stairs, his food spraying across several rows of players' family members. The tubby guy rolled all of the way down the aisle and somehow somersaulted right over the railing and onto the Red Sox dugout roof. He took out a $65,000 television camera, which shattered into a billion pieces that went raining down onto the field like some sort of cyborgian downpour.

Then the fat guy, the cameraman, and the last few chunks of camera went crashing over the side of the dugout and landed on top of Dustin Pedroia, the Red Sox's star second baseman, breaking his leg in three places and pretty much ending the Sox's play-off hopes.

Needless to say, this clip got tons of airtime on ESPN. They played it at least eight thousand times between all forty-six of their stations within the next twenty-four hours. The video went viral on the internet, getting over three million views faster than any other video in history. The fact that I'd been wearing Red Sox gear made the whole thing even worse.

Basically, I was a laughingstock. Not just of my school, but of the whole *country*. Plus, I got a black eye to remind everyone at school, or in the subway, or anywhere in public, every day for the next several weeks that I was, indeed, *that kid*.

"Hey, hey, aren't you *that kid*?" they'd all say anywhere I went in public before laughing hysterically and mimicking my infamous whiff.

Furthermore, Nate's elbow had basically shattered when he fell trying to hold me back. Which really sucks, because he was the school basketball team's star point guard. And even though the basketball season didn't start for a few months, his elbow wouldn't be fully healed until after the basketball season was over, essentially ending our chances of becoming the first team to ever win three straight regional championships. Mr. Benedict, the basketball coach, was also my Social Studies teacher, which meant I could pretty much kiss my chances at getting an A, or probably even a C, in his class good-bye.

And of course I lost the election for class president by a landslide. A combination of spilling soda on a popular girl, killing our basketball season before it even began, and just generally making a fool of myself while embarrassing the whole school can have that effect. I think the final tally was: me 11 votes, the other candidate 297 votes. I still to this day can't walk down the hall at school without people constantly throwing stuff at me and yelling, "Catch, butterfingers!" and then cracking some joke about me breaking people's limbs.

To make matters worse, another video clip from the game showed Derek Jeter in the dugout watching the replay on the Jumbotron and then smirking and laughing with his teammates. Instead of getting derided for such cruelty (I mean, he hit a little kid in the face with a baseball!), the talking heads on ESPN just laughed right along with him, citing his great sense of humor about it all.

But I haven't even told you the worst part. The worst part was what happened the evening after the game, right before the next game started. Because of the public reaction to what happened, Jeter agreed to do a meet-and-greet with me where he'd present me with a few autographed items and take some photos. I guess it was supposed to be an apology or something. Gatorade sponsored the event, and it got some media attention, but my name was hardly mentioned. Basically, all of the articles just went on and on about how great Derek Jeter was to forgive the poor unco-ordinated boy for causing such a scene and what a great person he was. He didn't even apologize to me personally during the entire ten-minute press conference. And I had to endure the angry stares of all the Red Sox fans in the room for wrecking Pedroia's leg. Not to mention the melt-ing glares the cameraman was giving me. Have you ever had to sit in a room with a bunch of grown-ups who all hate your guts? No? Well, let me tell you, it sucks.

And then some reporter guy asked me a question. "What's it like to get to meet Derek Jeter in person?"

I looked at him. And I looked at all the faces of the people around him. And I thought about the election, and Sara Hernandez, and the Red Sox's season, and the way Mr. Benedict looked at me in the hall that day for taking out his star player—the same way the Red Sox manager would probably look at me for taking out his star player, Pedroia. And I opened my mouth to answer. And then—I couldn't help it—I cried. And the room was silent, just the sound of me crying, and then, well . . . I peed my pants. I wish I was kidding, but you don't know what it was like. Have you ever had to sit in a room being forced to drink glass after glass of Gatorade while billions of cameras and microphones are pointed at you and making you relive the worst moment of your life over and over again in front of millions of viewers across the country? No? Well, okay then, maybe you would have peed yourself too, so shut up.

Of course, once that happened, Derek once again used my embarrassment for his own gain by cracking some joke about fish sticks that didn't even make sense but that everybody laughed at so hard you'd have thought it was the best joke ever told in history. At least they stopped paying attention to me after his joke.

Oh, and to cap it all off, Jeter hit a two-run home run on the very first pitch he saw that night and wound up scoring what would ultimately be the winning run.

And, remember, it had been my birthday.

Clearly, Derek Jeter had to pay.

*　*　*

A few weeks into Jeter's insane hot streak, which was also a few weeks after he was supposed to have been cursed, I decided that the baseball gods weren't going to let me deliver Jeter's comeuppance in the form of poor play on the field for some inexplicable reason. Probably Jeter sold his soul to them in the minors for eternal luck or something. Who knows?

Anyway, I decided I'd have to show everybody just what kind of person Jeter really is in another way. The perfect opportunity presented itself to me a few days later. Most kids were spending their weekends at the beach or something like that, enjoying the last few weeks of nice weather before fall really hit the coast, but I spent all my free time on the computer researching the best way to get back at Jeter. And I came upon something interesting on Saturday afternoon.

Derek Jeter was launching a new line of cologne as a part of some shameless sell-out million-dollar endorsement deal he'd made with Macy's. The cologne was called *Stolen*, probably in reference to the fact that sometimes opposing pitchers let Jeter steal bases out of pity. A more accurate name for it would have been *Hack* or *Overpaid* or *Worthless Jerk Who Everybody Loves for Some Reason Despite Being Nothing Better Than an Old Rusty Useless Puke Bucket*.

Anyway, the point is, I came up with the perfect plan to ruin his big perfume event and probably make him look like an idiot in the process. Shoot, maybe if I got really lucky, he'd slip on a chunk of poop and separate his shoulder or something. Oh, yes, the plan most definitely was going to involve feces. Lots of it, with any luck.

I just needed to convince Nate to help me.

"Why are we doing this again?" Nate asked.

"You know why."

"No, I mean, destroy Derek Jeter, yeah, I get that. I mean, what does my mom's business have to do with getting back at Derek Jeter?"

"You'll see," I said.

Nate sighed. "I don't like this."

"Yeah, well, you should be behind me on this. Derek Jeter is also responsible for your shattered elbow, remember?" I said.

It looked like Nate was going to disagree with me about that for some reason, but then he just sighed and handed me his mom's spare keys. We headed downstairs and then across the street to his mom's kennel. She runs a daycare business for dogs. It's crazy to me that people pay her to watch their dog while they're at work every day. I mean, seriously, can't you just leave your dog at home like most normal people? But I guess I should be happy that there are so many morons in New York City with extra cash and dogs. Because my plan wouldn't have been a plan at all without them.

We went around to the back door. It was lunchtime, which meant all of the dogs were in their little kennels or cages eating separately while Nate's mom was in her little office eating lunch herself and taking a break. Her assistant almost always left to go get lunch somewhere else.

I used the key Nate had given me, and we slipped in the back door. Luckily, the dogs were already crazily howling and barking, like always, so nobody heard us come in. We went into the back kennel area, and I grabbed a handful of leashes and got to work.

Ten minutes later, I had leashed up twenty-eight dogs of various sizes and breeds and was ready to head over to the event. Nate wanted to stay behind, partly because he wouldn't be much help with only one arm and partly because he was whining about how he was already grounded for two weeks and if he got caught doing this it'd probably become two years.

But I made him come with me for moral support. And to try and help control the dogs a little bit until we got there.

I knew twenty-eight dogs at once were going to be a challenge, but I really had no idea. Walking the dogs down Sixth Avenue toward the gigantic Macy's on Thirty-fourth did not actually happen. No, the truth was that they walked me down Sixth Avenue toward the gigantic Macy's on Thirty-fourth.

People screamed and dove out of the way as my herd of dogs barreled down the busy sidewalk. It was probably the mix of big and small, hairy and naked, peeing and pooping that caused the most staring. Also the barking. Oh, and the fact that there were twenty-eight all tethered to one little kid, while his friend with a broken arm in a sling ran behind them desperately shouting about what a terrible idea this was.

One guy in a suit shook his fist at me as we swarmed past him, and I gave him a shrug before being yanked by the force of 112 legs attached to twenty-eight leashes. I half expected my arm to come right out of its socket, leaving me behind in the dust. To prevent that, I just walked, or ran that is, at the dogs' pace.

But it was going to be worth it. I couldn't wait to see Jeter's face once I let this pack of crazed beasts loose onto his little event. There'd be shattered bottles of cologne everywhere, dogs barking, poop marinating in Derek Jeter's new scent. I could just see the headlines: DEREK JETER'S NEW COLOGNE SMELLS LIKE POOP, LITERALLY. I was pretty sure that most journalists would kill to get to use the words "poop" and "literally" in the same headline.

And Derek would be so shaken by the whole ordeal that he'd finally go into the deep slump I'd cursed him with last week. People would call it the Canine Curse, probably.

By the time we got to Macy's, the pack of dogs had amassed in their fur and mouths a nice amount of garbage and other junk they'd bowled through along the way. A Boston terrier and some sort of weird-looking naked miniature pinscher near the front of the pack were angrily fighting over a leather glove while a retriever beside them peed on a garbage can. This was going to be great, I could tell already.

I read that the event was going to be on the first floor, right near the main entrance on Thirty-fourth Street. Which would be perfect, since a kid with twenty-eight dogs probably wouldn't get too far into the store before being Tasered or something.

As soon as we got inside, I saw that a crowd had gathered and was snapping pictures like crazy as Derek Jeter held up a bottle of his cologne and smiled. His giant dimples looked so ridiculously deep and hungry that I thought one of them might try to take a bite out of a nearby journalist.

"So, what's the plan?" asked Nick. "We need to make sure that we can collect the dogs again and get them back to . . ."

"This is the plan," I said as I took some beef jerky out of my pockets and whistled to get the dogs' attention. I let go of their leashes and then threw the beef jerky right at Derek Jeter.

He caught the jerky in the air (lucky catch) and made a face as he recognized me. But a moment later he was buried by dogs. The room exploded with shouts, I heard the sound of breaking glass, and I knew my work here was done. I laughed and took off running, with Nate close behind me shouting about how we never should have done this. But he just didn't know a good revenge plot when he saw it. As much as I'd have loved to stick around and see the chaos, to see my brilliant plan working like a charm, I also didn't want to get caught.

"I'm out, I'm sorry," Nate said.

"What? Now? When we're so close to victory?" I had come over to his house to hopefully smooth things over with his mom for the whole dog thing. But we were out on the stoop, and it looked like he didn't even want to let me into his building.

"Look, you're losing your mind. And you got me grounded for *six months* for that dog stunt! I might not get to play basketball next year, either, at this rate. Plus, my mom might even lose her license! And where did it even get you anyway?"

He had a point. The fallout from the dogs was not what I'd expected. The whole thing had made headlines, of course, but not in the way I'd hoped. The next day there'd been a huge article in the *New York Times* about it, featuring a giant picture of Derek Jeter holding one small dog in one arm and hugging a huge Dalmatian with the other. I had stared at it for a long time, sure that his dimples were mocking me.

The article went on to glorify Derek Jeter as some kind of hero. I mean, sure, instead of freaking out, he actually ran all over the store helping to corral the dogs even though he could have just stood aside like most celebrities would have. But that still doesn't make him a hero, does it? And, yeah, maybe he did run out into the heavy traffic on Thirty-fourth to snag a little Yorkie terrier right before it got flattened. But still, I mean, if I had done that, I probably would have gotten stoned to death in Central Park as punishment for holding up traffic. But because it was Derek Jeter, he's now getting some sort of humanitarian award, and PETA was even quoted as saying, "Derek Jeter's the best thing that has happened to dogs since nonkill animal shelters were started."

And to top it all off, his cologne apparently got a ton of press and everyone bought it, and now I can't walk down the street without smelling *Stolen* wafting off every guy I pass.

What gives? He could do no wrong!

I just didn't get it. Derek Jeter could probably steal from poor people and then burn all their money right in front of them and roast a pig over the fire and not share any of it with them, and then, not only would people not be upset about it, but he would probably get awarded a Congressional Medal of Honor for it all.

It seemed the only way I could take down Jeter was to catch him in the act of doing something terrible. So that's exactly what I planned to do.

"Just this one last time, please. Then I'm done, I swear," I pleaded to Nate.

Nate sighed. "Wes, no. Let it go."

Just then a racquetball bounced off my head, and someone walking down the block said, "Catch, Shin-Breaker!" at least two full seconds after it had already hit me.

Nate grabbed the doorknob with his one good arm and slammed the door closed. I sat down on his stoop and wallowed. I thought I saw an image of Derek Jeter's face in the craggy concrete sidewalk the way some crazies claim to see Yogi Berra's face in their toast. I picked up a dirty plastic fork lying on the ground and started jabbing it into Jeter's face over and over again until all that was left gripped in my hand was a splintered chunk of dirty plastic.

The final plan would need to be epic. I mean, Derek Jeter had already made me the laughingstock of my school and ruined my chances of ever being class president or being able to get through a single day of middle school without getting taunted mercilessly. But since then he was now also pretty much responsible for me losing my last remaining friend. I hadn't thought he could make my life any worse than he had a couple months ago, but I guess there really is one thing that Derek Jeter is good at: destroying kids' lives.

So my next plan would need to be good. It had to work or else he would win like he always did. It also would need to involve a direct face-to-face meeting with Jeter. Luckily, I knew he had a soft spot for charities. It also helped that I had a lot of free time on my hands, thanks to having no friends and basically being a social leper at school.

Setting up a huge celebrity charity event isn't as hard as you'd think. For one, I knew how to contact Jeter's people due to the whole baseball-hitting-my-face incident that had started all of this. And I used the dog angle to hook him. I also called Nate's mom and, after apologizing profusely and promising to get her business some much-needed positive publicity, she agreed to help me set it up. You see, she would be one of the sponsors, along with PETA, the Humane Society, and several other animal charities. Nobody with a soul can say no to animal charities. Luckily for me, Derek Jeter was good at pretending to have a soul.

I challenged Jeter to a charity race between him and me around the bases at Yankee Stadium. The race would be for fun and entertainment; the real winners, as far as most people were concerned, would be the charities. But I knew better. People would still be interested in the outcome of the race. And I was going to win the race, by any means necessary, and expose him as the old, slow, washed-up player that he'd become.

The race was scheduled for right before Game 1 of the American League Division Series. Because Jeter had pretty much been the Yankees' star player ever since I'd placed that curse on him, he'd carried them right through to another appearance in the postseason. I think it was, like, the Yankees' nine hundredth play-off series, but who even knew anymore? They'd won (or purchased, really) too many to count.

I cursed Doctor Zanzubu Zardoz. He and his stupid voodoo Klingon magic would likely win Jeter another World Series and his first league MVP, and thus another record to go along with them. It was no wonder that Derek Jeter was in such a great mood the day of the race.

"Hey, how's the eye?" he said to me with a huge grin as we both approached home plate. People around us took pictures, the crowd cheered, and several kids with dogs on leashes near the dugout started chanting Jeter's name.

I scowled at him. I'd show him soon enough. I'd show them all.

There was some media there, but not as many reporters as you might think, as well as the charity sponsors, the corporate sponsors who would be providing the money to the charity of the winner. Nate was there, too, which had surprised me. I mean, given that his mom's kennel was one of the local sponsors and everything, it made some sense that he'd snag tickets to the game but he pretty much hated my guts now, or so he had implied when he decided to sit at another table by himself at lunch ever since the Macy's incident, so I was still surprised. He stared at me from his spot near the visitor's dugout, watching with a look on his face that I can only guess was morbid curiosity.

"Are you ready?" Jeter asked me with a smirk as we stretched on either side of home plate.

I said nothing. I could tell he wasn't taking this seriously. Well, he would be soon enough.

"Don't worry," he said. "I'll keep it close."

I scoffed at him.

What Jeter didn't know was that I'd been training for this nonstop for a week, running sprints in our apartment building hallway. Apparently, some neighbors eventually complained, and my parents were assessed a $250 fee. Just add that to the list of ways that Derek Jeter had screwed me over, I guess. But the point is, I was ready. I knew Derek wasn't going to take this seriously; and before he knew what was happening, I'd have won, making him look like a fool. Right then, standing next to Jeter, I needed to just beat him at *something*.

"Everybody ready?" the host asked.

We both nodded. Instead of firing a starter pistol in the air, they had arranged for the sound of a ball hitting a bat to be played over the PA. The sound played, and we were off.

I fired out of the starting gates like a rocket. My feet

had never moved faster. Heading into first base I was sure I had to have had like a ten-foot lead on him by now. As we rounded first, me on the inside and Jeter on the outside, I glanced over and saw that he was actually right next to me. I hadn't left him in the dust at all. He was keeping pace with me, and I could tell that it was incredibly easy for him. Even with his, like, forty-five-year-old-man legs, he was merely jogging lightly to stay on pace with me.

What had I been thinking? It didn't matter how many sprints I had done. He's a professional athlete. Of course he was going to be able to keep up with me. The truth hit me like a baseball bat cracking my forehead, and nothing could have made me angrier in that moment. He needed to look clumsy, washed up like an old dishrag named Gormley that had too many holes in it to be useful anymore. Instead, he was going to look like the guy who let a little kid win a silly race for charity. A hero. Just like he always did.

So I did the only thing I could think of to make him look foolish.

I tripped him.

We approached second base, and I swung my right foot over subtly in an attempt to clip his heel and make him fall flat on his face. And I did clip his heel. But it was like kicking a hunk of iron. He hardly missed a step, whereas I went flying face-first into second base.

The crowd gasped, and then some of them laughed. He'd done it again! I couldn't believe it. I lay motionless, facedown in the dirt, covered head to toe in embarrassment, listening to several thousand people shift awkwardly in their seats.

My life was over.

The crowd started applauding, and I looked toward home, expecting to see Jeter at the plate posing with the president's daughters and accepting a special citation from the United Nations for services to humanity or something. But he wasn't. He had stopped running and was standing next to me. He held out his hand.

"That was a pretty nice slide," he joked. "But the race doesn't end here."

I could tell from the look on his face, on the faces of everyone in attendance, that they knew I'd tried to intentionally trip him. And yet here he was, acting cool as a cucumber about it, like we were best pals. My initial gut reaction, which had been to reach out and slap his hand away and try to kick him in the shin, faded into the dirt underneath me.

And for the first time since the whole ordeal began, I think I finally made a good decision.

I grabbed his hand and let him help me up. I smiled at him and then laughed like it was all just some joke. And the crowd laughed like they were all in on it, like we were all best buddies. Jeter and I finished the race side by side, touching home at the same time.

Then Derek Jeter did what he does best, which is to be the most beloved figure in all of sports. He announced that he'd personally be matching all money given to all of the charities involved, and then doubling it.

As music started playing over the loudspeaker and the grounds crew started getting the field ready for the game, Jeter pulled me aside.

"Listen," he said, "I know you must still be pretty upset about the way that foul ball thing played out."

"How could you tell?"

He laughed. "Right, well, I just want you to know that I *am* sorry. For the way I reacted in the dugout and the way the whole thing played out for you. And I know you're a Red Sox fan, which I can deal with, but how about I hook you up with tickets to every Red Sox/Yankees game played here at the stadium for life?"

I couldn't keep the smile off my face. So I just smiled and nodded dumbly. Then I said, "I'm sorry, too."

Derek Jeter shrugged and smiled again, that stupid,

likable smile, and then he walked away.

"Nice race," someone behind me said.

I think Nate had meant for the comment to be sarcastic. But I just laughed and shrugged and said, "I think I've just realized something. Something huge."

"What's that?" Nate asked.

"That all of this hasn't really been Derek Jeter's fault after all. I mean, if I was down 0–2 in the count, I would have done the same thing. I'd have battled through every single pitch to keep the at bat alive. I can't blame Jeter for hitting a foul ball. And how could he have controlled where it was going to go, or what it was going to do, after he did?"

For the first time in . . . well, probably since *that* night, Nate grinned.

"I was wondering when you might figure that out," he said.

I nodded. "Yeah, and I think I'm beginning to finally realize whose fault the whole thing really is. I think I've known all along, deep down, but just didn't want to admit it to myself," I said.

"Good!" Nate said. "I'm glad you've finally realized that you've had no one to blame but yourself for all of this . . ."

"What!?" I said, shocked at his assumption. "No, not me!"

Nick gave me a look. I ignored him.

"This," I said, "was all Jon Lester's fault!"

Nate just stared at me.

"Yeah, this has all been Jon Lester's fault all along! That idiot kept throwing Jeter fastballs. I mean, who does that when you're up 0–2 in the count? It was Jon Lester who sparked the chain of events that ruined my social standing and made me the laughingstock of an entire country!"

I decided right then and there that Jon Lester must die.

I even announced it loudly with my finger pointed in the air to let everyone know I was serious, "I will destroy you, Jon Lester!"

≈ ABOUT ≈
GUYS╬READ

Guys Read sports stuff. And you just proved it. (Unless you just opened the book to this page and started reading. In which case, we feel bad for you because you missed some pretty awesome sports stuff.)

Now what?

Now we keep going—Guys Read keeps working to find good stuff for you to read, you read it and pass it along to other guys. Here's how we can do it.

For ten years, Guys Read has been at www.guysread.com, collecting recommendations of what guys really want to read. We have gathered recommendations for thousands of great funny books, scary books, action books, illustrated books, information books, wordless books, sci-fi books, mystery books, and you-name-it books.

So what's your part of the job? Simple: try out some of the suggestions at guysread.com, try some of the other stuff written by the authors in this book, then let us know what you think. Tell us what you like to read. Tell us what you don't like to read. The more you tell us, the more great book recommendations we can collect. It might even help us choose the writers for the next installment of Guys Read.

Thanks for reading.

And thanks for helping Guys Read.

JON SCIESZKA (editor) has been writing books for children ever since he took time off from his career as an elementary school teacher. He wanted to create funny books that kids would want to read. Once he got going, he never stopped. He is the author of numerous picture books, middle grade series, and even a memoir. From 2007–2010 he served as the first National Ambassador for Children's Literature, appointed by the Library of Congress. Since 2004, Jon has been actively promoting his interest in getting boys to read through his Guys Read initiative and website. Born in Flint, Michigan, Jon now lives in Brooklyn with his family. Visit him online at www.jsworldwide.com and at www.guysread.com.

SELECTED TITLES

THE TRUE STORY OF THE THREE LITTLE PIGS
(Illustrated by Lane Smith)

THE STINKY CHEESE MAN AND
OTHER FAIRLY STUPID TALES
(Illustrated by Lane Smith)

The Time Warp Trio series,
including SUMMER READING IS KILLING ME
(Illustrated by Lane Smith)

The Spaceheadz series

DUSTIN BROWN ("Against All Odds") is the captain and right wing for the NHL's Los Angeles Kings. Dustin was drafted in the first round (13th overall) by the Kings in the 2003 draft, when he was just eighteen years old. Over the course of his nine-year career, Dustin has played for the US Olympic team, been named an NHL All-Star, and became the youngest captain in the history of the Los Angeles Kings organization. He lives in California with his wife and three sons.

JAMES BROWN ("The Choice") has been a sports anchor and broadcaster for almost twenty years. He is best known as the host of *The NFL Today* on CBS and the acclaimed *Inside the NFL* on Showtime. Prior to this, J. B. was a college basketball star at Harvard, achieving All-Ivy League honors in three of his four seasons. J. B. lives in Maryland with his family.

SELECTED TITLE

ROLE OF A LIFETIME: *Reflections on Faith, Family, and Significant Living* (With Nathan Whitaker)

JOSEPH BRUCHAC ("Choke") is a Native American poet, novelist, and musician. He has written more than 120 books for children and adults, and has been honored with the Virginia Hamilton Literary Award and the Jane Addams Book Award, among others. He lives in the foothills of the Adirondack Mountains in New York State. Find out more at www.josephbruchac.com.

SELECTED TITLES

WOLF MARK

CODE TALKER: *A Novel About the Navajo Marines of World War Two*

THIRTEEN MOONS ON TURTLE'S BACK
(With Jonathan London;
Illustrated by Thomas Locker)

CHRIS CRUTCHER ("The Meat Grinder"), a recipient of NCTE's National Intellectual Freedom Award, the ALAN Award, the ALA's Margaret A. Edwards Award for Lifetime Achievement, and the CLA's St. Katharine Drexel Award, is the author of fifteen books for young readers. Prior to writing, Chris taught school in Washington and California. He lives in Spokane, Washington. You can find him online at www.chriscrutcher.com.

SELECTED TITLES

WHALE TALK

CHINESE HANDCUFFS

RUNNING LOOSE

TIM GREEN ("Find Your Fire") was a star linebacker for the Atlanta Falcons and an NFL analyst for FOX Sports before turning his talents to writing. He has written more than twenty books for kids and adults, including the *New York Times* bestseller FOOTBALL GENIUS, about which football legend Bill Parcells said, "as close as you can come to NFL action without putting on the pads." He lives with his wife and children in upstate New York. You can read more about Tim at www.timgreenbooks.com.

SELECTED TITLES

FOOTBALL GENIUS

BASEBALL GREAT

UNSTOPPABLE

DAN GUTMAN ("How I Won the World Series") has written eleven baseball-card adventure novels, including HONUS & ME, JACKIE & ME, and BABE & ME. He has also written about sports in THE MILLION DOLLAR SHOT, THE MILLION DOLLAR KICK, THE MILLION DOLLAR GOAL, THE MILLION DOLLAR PUTT, and THE MILLION DOLLAR STRIKE. You can visit him at www.dangutman.com.

SELECTED TITLES

THE KID WHO RAN FOR PRESIDENT

THE HOMEWORK MACHINE

The Genius Files, including:
Book One: MISSION UNSTOPPABLE

GORDON KORMAN ("The Trophy") has written more than seventy middle grade and teen novels. Favorites include the *New York Times* bestselling The 39 Clues: Cahills vs. Vespers, Book One: THE MEDUSA PLOT. Gordon lives with his family on Long Island, New York. You can visit him online at www.gordonkorman.com.

SELECTED TITLES
UNGIFTED

POP

SCHOOLED

SHOWOFF

CHRIS RYLANDER ("I Will Destroy You, Derek Jeter") is the author of the Fourth Stall saga. He is a fan of pointy wizard hats, blind squirrels, and the Chicago Cubs. He lives in Chicago with his wife and dog. Check out more at www.chrisrylander.com.

SELECTED TITLES

THE FOURTH STALL

THE FOURTH STALL PART II

THE FOURTH STALL PART III

ANNE URSU ("Max Swings for the Fences") is the acclaimed author of BREADCRUMBS, as well as the three middle grade novels that comprise the Cronus Chronicles trilogy. Anne is also a professor of writing for children at Hamline University and a lifelong Minnesota Twins fan. She lives in Minneapolis with her son and three cats. Visit her at www.anneursu.com.

SELECTED TITLES

BREADCRUMBS

The Cronus Chronicles:
Book One: THE SHADOW THIEVES
Book Two: THE SIREN SONG
Book Three: THE IMMORTAL FIRE

JACQUELINE WOODSON ("The Distance") is the author of more than twenty books for young readers—picture books, middle grade books, and teen novels. Her books have received numerous honors, including a Coretta Scott King Honor, National Book Award finalist, Newbery Honors, and a Margaret A. Edwards Award for Lifetime Achievement. Read more about her at www.jacquelinewoodson.com.

SELECTED TITLES

LOCOMOTION

MIRACLE'S BOYS

FEATHERS

DAN SANTAT (illustrator) is a writer and illustrator of many, many things. In addition to writing and drawing many books for kids, he has provided artwork for the *Wall Street Journal*, *Esquire*, and *Time Out Kids*. He also created the hit Disney Channel cartoon *The Replacements*. Dan lives in California with his wife, two kids, and many pets. Find out more at www.dantat.com.

SELECTED TITLES

SIDEKICKS

GUILD OF GENIUSES

OH NO! OR, HOW MY
SCIENCE PROJECT DESTROYED THE WORLD
(Written by Mac Barnett)

Jon Scieszka presents
THE GUYS READ LIBRARY
OF GREAT READING

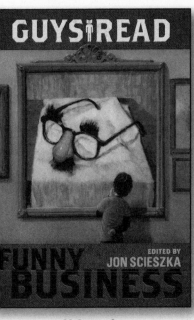

Volume 1

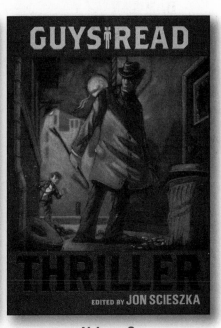

Volume 2

What more could a guy ask for?

WALDEN POND PRESS™
An Imprint of HarperCollinsPublishers

www.harpercollinschildrens.com